Secret Santa

Rebel Wayfarers MC
Book #9.75

MariaLisa deMora

First Published 2016

ISBN 13: 978-0-9983267-1-9

DEDICATION

*The afternoon knows what the morning
never suspected.*
~ Robert Frost

For those of us who long for love and companionship in our afternoons. Sometimes we simply need a reminder to keep the faith. That love is not something you discover. It cannot be acquired or invented. Love will come looking for you when you are ready. Be happy, and be hopeful. I see good things.

Contents

ACKNOWLEDGMENTS

Wanna know a secret? For reals? Okay. In this story, I'm Vanna. Big secret, right? My road name, CB radio handle, trail name, and nickname is Peepers. I hike, love to help people, hate to ask for help, and am a single mom to a special needs son with autism. So totally Vanna. Ta dah! Like you didn't already know it. Pfffttt.

Christmas Eve this past year was classically tough, with my minion having meltdowns over nothing and everything; some for reasons I knew, and many more I couldn't decipher. Around midnight, I was seated on my couch, reading, waiting for his tossings and turnings in the bed overhead to stop so I could put out the overfilled stocking, and deal with the cookies and milk. Within couple of weeks from writing this note, I'll be doing the same again this year. Yup, at 22-years-old, he still half believes in Santa, and I won't be the one to break *that* news to him. As long as he believes, Santa will come. Promise.

Last year, I spun up some old-school Christmas songs, thinking they would help pass the time. Those songs evoke sentimentality on a primal level, and within a matter of minutes I was driven to what seems to be my coping go-to these days: I grabbed the computer and opened a fresh, new document. And I wrote.

It felt good as I settled Vanna and Kitt. Helping them find their way through Kitt's growing adulthood, stamping the developmental changes into place that I know so well. By about 5 a.m., I had pretty much solidified Truck in my head, as well as on the page. He roared in and took control in places, and I gotta say, I love how he is with Vanna and Kitt. Truck enjoys a kind of intuitive empathy I wish everyone had.

I might be Vanna, but my minion isn't Kitt. Not quite. As my son has aged into a deeper emotional and cognitive maturity, he has developed the ability to articulate how it felt when things were more difficult. He can talk about the workings in his brain, feelings he experienced when his body reacted to certain stimuli, how he self-soothed, and the satisfaction felt as he developed independent coping mechanisms. There are bits of him in this story, of course, but Kitt wound up more profoundly impacted on the Autism spectrum which means a lot of Kitt's inner dialogue might be flavored by my son, but is straight from the source of my imagination.

I cannot speak for every parent or caregiver of a special needs child, but I know I long for the day when my son can be more independent. Not for me, but for *him*. He definitely recognizes how his age peers have moved along, passed him on the road to adulthood, and impatiently waits to join their journey. Emphatically and loudly, *he wants more*. And he'll get there, I have faith.

One of the toughest things about being a parent, regardless of the abilities of the child, is giving them the opportunity to branch out and flourish. Because with each opportunity to succeed, comes the same chance to fail. I keep reminding myself of a poem by the young Australian writer, Erin Hanson, *What If I Fall?* It's a short bit of poetry, but is poignant in a way that resonates with me. Five lines long, but rich in meaning, it ends in a voice filled with hope, "Oh but my darling, What if you fly?"

My Christmas wish? Here's hoping all our fledglings soar.

Woofully yours,

~ML

Chapter One

Truck

"Aw, what in the hell…" Turning off the highway and onto the country road, Truck rolled his bike to a stop, staring at the large wooden sign planted not twenty feet away. BRIDGE OUT was written in block letters across the top, while the just as ominous ROAD CLOSED was printed out across the bottom. *What in the fuck am I supposed to do now?* He was mentally strangling his direction-giving and house-selling friend back in Texas.

Pulling out his phone he looked at the display, shoving it back into his pocket at the message of no service. *Fuck.* While computing the time it would take to detour back to the small town up the road, he eyed the moon hanging overhead in the sky and decided to take a chance. His new house might be on this side of the bridge, after all.

Idling up the road, he was appreciative of the isolated slices of landscape glimpsed in the washed out glow from his headlight. Trees crowded the road, pines still in full coverage. Black in this light, but he knew if seen under the midday sun, that same canopy would glow green. A few hardwood trees, their branches bare, leaves piled in the ditch in bow breaks, testifying to the speed of a recent rain runoff.

A mailbox planted next to a right-hand driveway captured his attention and he saw a tidy house set slightly back from the road. Even at this late hour, the downstairs windows glowed from within, testifying to the insomnia of the occupants, perhaps. Twinkling lights adorned a tree in what was probably the front parlor or dining room. Welcoming and cozy, a home.

Not quite a mile down the road he sighted a driveway leading off the other side of the road and slowed. Moonlight shone down on a two-story farmhouse set in the middle of a clearing. Darkness ringed the edges and there were no lights from the house to push back the shadows. The realtor's sign placed prominently near the sideways sagging mailbox proudly proclaimed SOLD.

A twist of his handlebars caused his lights to flash across the front, a temporary illumination shucked off

MariaLisa deMora

as easily as rain from a duck's back. Rolling to a stop he looked at the house as he killed the engine, blank windows giving him nothing back. Fitting accommodations for a man determined to go it alone, needing nothing more than a secluded place where he could lay up for a while, lick his wounds. Old wounds, but that didn't mean they didn't still bleed. Silence flooded the space around him as the noise from the bike died. Isolation, solitude, and privacy. His new house.

SECRET SANTA

Chapter Two

Vanna

The smooth, dulcet tones of Nat King Cole rolled out of the speakers and Savannah Reicht settled her head more comfortably against the back of the chair. Fingers plucking at the fabric-covered arms, she slowly relaxed and allowed her eyes to sink closed. Echoing strings held the melody of 'The Christmas Song' together through the bridge and she found herself softly mouthing the words about simple things others took for granted during the holiday season. Open fires, family activities, and childhood joys. *Now, you're just being maudlin*, she thought as the song wound down to silence. *Mister Cole would frown on maudlin thoughts on Christmas Eve.*

The scratching needle on the record signaled the beginning of the next song and she smiled to hear Dean's voice sliding through the room. He would have her dreaming of a 'White Christmas,' something that seldom happened down here in northern Florida. Reaching for the glass of wine sitting on the table beside the lamp, she leaned over and with her other hand picked up the open book lying there. Easing back into the chair, she shifted slightly and tucked one foot underneath her bottom before moving to find the ultimate comfy position. Her wine glass balanced on one thigh, elbow to the chair's arm, the book lifted to the level of her eyes.

It had been a busy and stressful few days. A race to get the last of the presents wrapped, boxed, and mailed off in time for a pre-holiday delivery for those of her friends living far away. Her gaze flicked up and she glanced across the room, staring for a moment at the tree standing in one corner of her dining room. Brilliant, the tree was covered in multi-colored lights and tinsel carelessly tossed by the handfuls. The homemade felt skirt underneath littered with bright packages and bags, while one stuffed-full stocking lay on its side nearby.

Only a few of the packages under the tree were from her, and she knew in his quiet way Kitt would appreciate the efforts of those who sent presents for him. Kitt was her son, now a young adult. Living at home wasn't what he wanted—and given the development of his independent streak a mile wide over the past couple of years, wouldn't be something she'd have forever—but him living at home was what they had, for now.

She knew she would eventually be able to find a good living arrangement for him, one that hit all the tick marks on her list, but not this year. She still had life lessons to teach, and Kitt responsibilities to accept, duties to carry out. So this year she still had him at home, and felt blessed that he was at this moment upstairs, sleeping in bed—even if his journey to that bed had been conducted under protest tonight—and waiting for Santa's appearance. Baby steps.

Vanna sighed, looking back at the words on the page and used the edge of her thumb to flip forward in her book. The unconscious movement of her hand allowed her imagination free rein to advance through the story, and she was quickly caught back up in the foibles of a dense-as-mud heroine. One shoulder of her oversized t-shirt slipped off her shoulder as she lifted the glass of blush liquid to her lips, and she adjusted the shirt with practiced ease. She sipped the wine, shivering slightly at the still-chilled temperature.

Vanna and Kitt lived alone; the few visitors they had these days were expected and scheduled. Known and quantified. No surprises, not ever. With Kitt's disorder it was important his environment be tightly managed and controlled. While the reality was he was autistic, she liked to say that on the spectrum he was blessedly high-functioning. Which meant he was both verbal and cognitively advanced, which further meant he could communicate important things. And that meant he could also argue the paint off a fencepost when he was in the mood to want something. Like tonight, with his pleas for just one more story, one more cartoon, one more snack. It was only the threat of Santa bypassing the houses of boys who weren't good that scooted his feet up the stairs and into bed.

She sighed, the past few days had seen a retreat in his behaviors. She knew it was likely just stress from the holiday's change in routine putting him off balance in a way that came out as combative. With these kids, nothing was 'just,' though. He had lost much of his language, retaining only a few of his most-used words, and she had watched him withdrawing more every day, even from contact with her.

Vanna desperately wanted him to have memories to draw on for future Christmases. She struggled to balance the need to give him sameness with her desire to create a wealth of experiences he could use to better offset stress as he moved through life. Each moment offered learning opportunities, and she spent a great deal of time working with him to develop scripts and coping mechanisms. Beginning in early December, they went over the game plan every day, talking through the process of buying and wrapping presents. Decorating the tree required a conversation all its own, as did gift opening protocol. She knew all this work wasn't about making Christmas merry for him this year, but an attempt to make it less difficult for him in ten years, or twenty.

My whole life is an evolving script, she thought, putting down the book, giving up on the romance novel when it failed to retain her attention. She let her mind swirl and pick at the past few days, trying to find her own balance. She wasn't wrong about the scripting, because much of her time spent with Kitt was angled with an eye towards what he would need in the future. She wouldn't be around forever. *There you go again, that's another maudlin thought*. She sighed at herself, taking another sip of wine. *True, though. And if something happened to me…*when *something happens, there are only a few people Kitt would trust enough.*

As she often did, she began making a list in her head, only half listening as the record transitioned to the last track on the holiday album. When the music began to play she paused, smiling as Perry Como brought the holidays home with a reminder that the season meant family and friends. As he sang, the smile faded from her lips and she felt the stinging at the back of her eyes that was all-too familiar this time of year. *I wish for a Merry Christmas, too. A Christmas with friends, family…a lover.* She sighed. *At least I have Kitt*, she reminded herself, trying to shake off the tears, swallowing hard against the lump choking her throat, ignoring how very empty the house felt.

Kitt's father hadn't handled the diagnosis well, and their marriage quickly became one of many dreams that fell as a casualty to autism. Her ex had quickly remarried—happily or unhappily, she didn't know and didn't really care. Other than to be annoyed at times that he had moved on so fast, believing it meant the relationship they had before Kitt mattered less because of it. *Which makes me feel like a fool*, she thought, swallowing again, *because I loved him.*

A low rumble edged into the room, grabbing her attention. Her isolated home sat on the outskirts of town, positioned alongside a copse of hardwood trees, somewhat rare in this section of the state. The sound grew until it enveloped her little house, windows shaking in their frames for a few moments. She watched through the front windows as headlights slashed through the night, flickering across the outside of her house before continuing on their way.

Odd, she thought, because there was hardly any traffic on her road during the day, much less at night. *Someone must be lost. I'm sure I'll see their lights headed back out in a minute or two.*

The narrow blacktop road dead-ended about a mile past her home. There was only one other house on the road, and once the excitement of the bridge washing out a couple years ago faded, there was nothing to warrant travelers to where the little creek meandered around the backside of her property.

That house, on the market now for more than a decade, once belonged to the uncle of a good friend, but the owner had been dead longer than the house had been for sale. *Maybe Blackie sold the place*, she thought. Just one more line on her mental list of things-to-do and she made a note to ask him about it when she talked to him in the morning. He and his wife Peaches were one of a half a dozen calls she would make once Kitt got up. Handling the frightening first contact to ensure there'd be no misdials or identification missteps. Waiting for his signal all was well, then passing the phone off to him so he could express his thanks for the gifts in safety. She, in turn, would receive thanks from their children, all five of whom she loved dearly.

Blackie had been a friend when she needed one in the worst way, and they had stayed in touch through the years. He had saved her in so many ways; she would be forever grateful, not just for what he had done, but for his continued friendship. Months could go by between calls and yet, when they talked, it seemed as if they saw each other every day. *I love him so hard*, she thought, shifting in her chair. She suddenly realized that, for a while now, she had been listening to the skritching crackle of the record needle circling the inner grooves of the album. Setting down her glass, she shook her head.

"Time for bed, chickie," she said softly, pushing up from the chair and turning to where the record player sat on top of the entertainment center. She reached and turned off the player at the same time she grabbed the empty record sleeve from where it leaned against the player. Record safely stowed, she had just turned to retrieve her glass and book when her front entryway echoed with knocking on the door. Not just knocking, but nearly a pounding that quickly, thankfully, ceased. "What the hell..."

Glancing out the front window, she saw the silhouette of a body outlined from the security light on a pole across the driveway from the house. The intent of the light was to cast a welcoming and safe-feeling circle of light on the yard and drive. While it was successfully doing that, it failed to illuminate the porch very well, which meant she could only see the outline of the body standing and facing away from her door.

A man, large and broad, clothes dark, hair glinting in the light, either silver or blond. A man, on her front porch—she glanced at the clock on the front of the DVR—at eleven at night. A man she didn't know—she looked beyond him at the empty driveway—with no apparent mode of transportation. He twisted at the waist, turning to look at her front door and she caught a glimpse. Not enough to really see his face, unless you counted what appeared to be look of frustration and anger telegraphed by the squinting of his eyes and twisted, tight line of his lips seen in silhouette.

He moved then, one arm stretching out to again pound at her door no doubt, that motion halted when he caught sight of her through the window. Leaning in, his upper torso entered the light cast from her living room lamps and her breath caught for a moment. *Beautiful,* was the first thought to enter her mind, then she corrected herself, murmuring, "No, too rugged. He's flat-out handsome."

"Hey," he called, lips stretching wide to part his full white and grey beard in a smile probably meant to reassure. *If that's what he's going for, it's working*, she thought. "It's late, I know it's late. *God*, I know it's late and I hate being the weird guy on your porch in the middle of the night. But, can you help me out?" One corner of his mouth quirked up, lifting the mustache on that side. "I got to my new place, but there's no phone. I'm a couple days early for electric, even. And to top it off, I ain't got no service out here." At this he lifted one hand, a cellphone engulfed in his grip, and waggled it back and forth. "Might as well be holdin' a brick," he said, and then scoffed and she watched as his shoulders lifted in a shrug that communicated a 'whacha gonna do' statement.

He took a single stride towards the window, head now cocked to one side. She saw his hair was long, caught behind his head in a ponytail the end of which had flipped over his shoulder. White, to match his beard. "Hey, miss? Miss? Can you hear me?"

Miss? The startled thought flitted through her head just before she lifted her chin and lowered it, offering him a single nod.

"Beauty," he said, those lips splitting the beard in another smile. "Gonna help me out?"

Now that he was closer, she saw he was wearing a black leather vest, something she recognized as biker gear. She had some experience in the garments worn by men who rode motorcycles, seeing as her Blackie was one, the president of the Freed Riders back home in Texas. Then, the daughter of her heart, Sharon, had married one, too. Gunny was a Rebel Wayfarers member, based out of Fort Wayne, Indiana, but their club had chapters in several states.

Studying the front of this man's vest she saw he had several rally patches sewn in what appeared to be a random order across the bottom edges. They spanned more than a decade, and the oldest looked the part, grime covered with long exposure.

The important patches were affixed high on either side of his chest in positions of honor. Illustrations of worth made from fabric and thread, displayed for everyone to see. A narrow rectangle with the letters 'SAA,' standing for sargent at arms was attached on his left side, over his heart, showing he held the club's trust in a title close. Respectful. Two patches on the right-hand side. Another rectangle with 'Truck,' positioned with a smaller 'Unka Tonk' underneath it. That one had a small rose next to the words, a detail that made her smile, because it spoke to his tolerance of whoever had gifted him with the patch. A child? Perhaps a lover. Someone loved, that was certain.

Her gaze returned to his face where his features had settled into unhappy lines. He had caught her looking at his vest, and now clearly expected zero assistance. *Hell*, she thought, *he's probably expecting me to throw up shutters to lock myself in and him out.* "Be right there," she called and was immediately rewarded by the glint of his teeth as he grinned broadly at her.

"Beauty," he said again, stepping back and turning to face the door.

She detoured past her purse hanging off the back of one of the dining room chairs, pulling her cell from the inside pocket. Her hand hesitated over the canister of mace, but then she remembered his smile and that patch, and shook her head, turning instead to pull open the inside door. He stood well back from the screen, slouching in an effort to not seem so…big. She had seen Gunny take this stance often enough and just the thought of the big ex-Marine made her smile, so when she flipped on the porchlight that grin was still on her face.

15

Chapter Three

Truck

Fuck me, Peter Teravest thought as the woman stepped onto the boards of the porch outside her front door. Through the window she had looked wary, but pretty and sweet. She hadn't seemed frightened by his unexpected appearance, which made him grateful because maybe, just maybe, she'd help a brother out. Now, standing in the bright light shining down from over the doorway, a warm smile illuminating her face from within, he saw she wasn't merely pretty, the woman was beautiful.

Thick auburn hair, streaked in only a few places with a lighter color. With her hair drawn back into a tight bun it was hard to decide if the coloring was natural or from time in a chair somewhere. *Love to see that hair down*, he thought, his imagination setting it swinging on either side of her face. Strong face, high cheekbones and arching eyebrows framed gorgeous green eyes. He'd place her age as somewhere between legal and about ten shy of his fifty years.

Just my fuckin' luck, he thought, careful to keep his internal grouse from his face, *I move to the middle of no-fucking-where on Christmas Eve and find myself landing next door to the county's beauty queen*. He didn't date, didn't have any desire for a relationship. Not anymore. *Not since...*

Aloud, he gave her his club name, saying, "I'm Truck, miss. Thank you for this. If I don't check in, I'll get my ass in hot water for sure." Smile fading from her face, she hadn't yet offered him the phone clutched in her hand. He stood there for a minute, awkwardly waiting. After another minute, when she still hadn't spoken or moved, he called a careful question. "Miss?"

With a jerk she lifted her arm, phone dangling from her fingers as she said, "Yes. Sorry. A moment." She pulled it back, did something to the screen, pressed her finger a time or two then held the device out again.

No ring on her finger. *Not that I'm lookin'*, he thought.

"Here you go, unlocked and the phone app is loaded. Just dial and you'll get your ass out of that hot water." She smiled broadly, humor evident in her sparkling eyes as she introduced herself, "Vanna. My friends call me Vanna. Pleased to meet you, Truck."

Accepting the phone, he carefully avoided brushing her fingers, not needing to know what her skin felt like. Another tactic he had employed for years, a way to keep people at bay. "Vanna," he acknowledged her name quietly. Truck liked that she didn't question the name he used, and as he dialed he mused about why that felt nice. Different, but nice. A moment of ringing then he heard a woman's voice, thick with amusement as she said, "Cock house, only roosters need apply. Whacha need?" Laughter echoed in the background, and he heard the sound of a palm lightly smacking flesh, then a man answered the phone, still laughing. "You got Red, whacha need?"

Good, someone I know, he thought, as his chin came up, shoulders relaxing from a tension he didn't even know he carried. "Red, man. It's Truck."

"Truck, long time no speak, brother." The warmth flooding his friend's voice made him grin. Based out of the Little Rock chapter, Truck had been out on one run or another for most of the past year. It was good to hear the brotherhood they held between them ran as deep and strong as ever. "Where the fuck are you this time?"

"Florida, man. Bought me a house." Vanna made a noise beside him and he watched her retreat to the door, murmuring a quiet, "I'll just give you some privacy," as she went back inside. He kept his eyes on her through the glass, and then through the living room windows as she walked to a chair by the back wall. She leaned over, her jeans stretching tight over her ass and he took a good, long look, tracing her curves with his eyes. *Beauty.* Straightening, she held a book and a glass in her hands, and he tracked her across the room, past the door where he lost her as she went deeper into the house.

With a start he realized Red had been talking to him, but he hadn't heard a word, totally engrossed in watching Vanna move. *So fucking beautiful.* Grunting agreement at the instruction to call in more often, he listened as the call disconnected, but kept the phone lifted, camouflaging his focused attention on the inside of Vanna's house.

Pictures on the wall of her and a boy, some scenic shots taken from high on a hillside, and—he leaned closer—several pictures of her with men in black leather vests, very much like the one he wore. None of her and a single man, though.

"Done with the phone?" So focused was he on cataloging her life, trying to discover if she had a man or not, he hadn't heard the screen door open. She was standing just inside, looking up, holding the door open, but not reaching for the phone. "Put it on the table if you are. If you have more calls to make, you are welcome to do that, as well. I was just making myself a sandwich, and it struck me that if you don't have telephone or electricity at your new home, then you might not have groceries, either. I've plenty, and if you are okay with plain fare, and by that I mean straight ham and cheese, I'm happy to send you home with at least a meal." Stepping back, the door began to close. "Take your time, and no offense taken if you've already eaten, I know it's late."

What in the hell? Tipping his head to one side, he reached out and halted the fall of the door to the frame, pulling it wide. "I'm starved, actually, Vanna. Everything in town was closed when I rolled through, so I haven't had anything since I ate breakfast early this morning. This is certainly my lucky day. My lucky day moving in next to a beautiful miss who's also thoughtful." He frowned at her self-deprecating snort and followed her into the house and through the dining room, pausing to place the phone on the table as requested.

She moved ahead of him to the kitchen at the back of the house and he took another long, appreciative look at her ass in those jeans. Enough woman to hold onto, plenty to cuddle up to if a man was so inclined. His cock thickened, surging to half-mast and he mentally told himself, *Down, boy.*

He turned to hide evidence of his arousal, taking a moment to look into the living room. He stared at the framed images of her at what looked to be a bike club's hog roast, squinting to see if he knew any faces in the picture. The frozen moments she chose to display on her walls were interesting. The fact they were framed meant the pictures were important to her, because people didn't take the time or spend money in order to hang an image that was throwaway. He stopped, squinting at one of the men standing, arm around her shoulder. *Fuck, I know him...*

One step, then another, and he was close enough to be certain of the man's identity. *Gunny. Fuck me.* Scanning the picture, he saw plenty of other faces he knew, too. It looked like half the Fort Wayne chapter was in this picture; every face turned towards her held a welcoming expression. Gunny's woman, Sharon, had her arms around the woman's waist, tucking herself tight against Vanna's side. *Interesting.* Intending to ask her about her association with the Rebels, he turned to walk to the kitchen only to pull up short. She was standing a few feet behind him, and he knew she'd gotten a look at his back patch from the look of startled recognition on her face.

"You're a Rebel," she said quietly, more a statement than a question and he stared at her.

Then, with a chin lift, he acknowledged what appeared to be her status with the club. Friend of the club. A trusted friend, based on what he saw in the picture. One of few non-family folks invited to a wedding held in the backlot behind the Fort's clubhouse last year. He hadn't been there, but had seen all the pictures posted to social media of Hoss kissing Hope, her swollen belly between them, her boy beside them. Instant family, something his brother needed for a long time without even knowing it. Vanna was a friend of the club, which meant even if he was so inclined, she wasn't available for a romp. Not even if they found themselves graced with a mutual attraction.

Glancing around, he stopped for a moment as he stared at the other picture, surprised to recognize this group, too. Blackie standing next to his old lady, Peaches, with Vanna, head thrown back in laughter, while lounging on a blanket to one side of the pool in Blackie's backyard. The Texas-based Freed Riders were friendly with the Rebels, and she had somehow bridged the gap between the two clubs, finding what looked like firm footing in both camps.

That was a feat, even for someone accustomed to navigating the political waters ever rough between clubs. Dark swirls concealing sinkholes around territory claims and members' egos; hell, even the color of a club's patch could be fast-flowing fodder for arguing. Yet here she was in two pictures...in two camps, laughing, friendly and comfortable.

Damn, I want to know more about this woman, he thought, gaze lingering for a moment on the picture, tracing over her charms exposed by the modest swimsuit worn as she lay in the brilliant Texas sunshine.

As he finished turning, his gaze fell on an old-fashioned record player placed on top of the oak cabinet in the corner that held her TV and accompanying electronic equipment. Putting aside all his questions, he looked over at her and asked with a grin, "Vanna, are you a closet vinyl fanatic?" Chuckling at her happy nod, he reached out and then paused, waiting politely to ask, "May I? I'd love to hear the wax poetic tonight."

At her softly voiced, "Yes, of course," he lifted the cover, noting the record-filled cardboard sleeves stacked nearby. With pleasure, he saw the top selection was a Christmas album, and retrieved it to place on the platter. Lifting the tonearm and holding his breath in anticipation, he set the needle carefully at the outer edge of the grooves pressed into the wax.

Silence for a moment, then soft chiming led into the timeless words of 'Silver Bells' sung by Jerry Vale. "Oh, darlin', I approve." He looked at her, seeing that gentle smile still in place on her full lips and he couldn't help himself. Extending his hand, he told her, "Dance with me. You have to, Vanna. It's practically a law, darlin'. A waltz demands it."

Her laughter filled the air and he abruptly found it hard to breathe because hearing it struck a chord deep inside him. Seeing the look on her face in the picture as she laughed was beautiful, but hearing it...*oh God*...hearing it was stunning.

She reached to grasp his hand and settled in, palm to palm. He used the connection to pull her closer, settling his other hand firmly on her back. Looking down, he moved, swaying to the music, the simple box step of the waltz not requiring much of his attention. That stayed firmly on the woman leaning so trustingly into him, her form nestled tight. He gripped her hand in warning, and then used it to push and turn her, twirling her out and then with the same grip drew her back, her hand slipping familiarly into place along his shoulder when she was pressed against his front again.

So beautiful, he thought, and without thinking started to serenade Vanna by merely mouthing the words, slowly segueing into a soft croon, singing along with Vale about how Christmas felt. She stared up at him, lips slightly parted, still tipped in that gentle smile. He tugged her a little closer as they slowly stepped in a measured square around her living room, rising and falling in time with the music.

Time felt suspended in that instant, a beautiful woman in his arms, chin tilted so she could smile up at him. Their bodies moving together, synchronized, as if they danced together every Christmas Eve like this. *I wish...*

The song slowly faded away and he tightened his arms, wanting to hold onto this for another moment. Then the next song began playing and she pulled in a breath that hitched in the middle, shaking herself slightly, clearly putting off the shared spell they had been under for too short a time.

Stepping back and pulling away, she gently forced his arms to release their hold. Her expression was solemn as she told him, "Thank you, Truck. That will be a beautiful memory for many Christmases to come." She leaned forward, flattening one palm in the center of his chest and he felt her touch like a brand on his skin. For one moment thinking she intended to kiss him, the idea heating him to his core. This meant something to her, and he found himself willing to expend any energy needed to discover what that was. Vanna was an intriguing woman, sweet and unassuming. Highlighting his thoughts, sincerity scored through her features as she fervently repeated, *"Thank you."*

Chapter Four

Vanna

What in the hell am I thinking? Thoughts were flying fast and furious through her head as she turned to the kitchen. She was suddenly hell bent on making large platters of sandwiches and getting a counter—*or better yet, an entire state*—between her and this man before she embarrassed herself further. *First I invite him in for a quick bite*—she shivered as her mind turned to his teeth scraping along her neck—*Stop it, Savannah.*

She opened the refrigerator; the cool air welcome as it caressed her heated cheeks. Quickly pulling out packages of meat and cheese, as well as condiment selections, she twisted to place them on the countertop only to run into Truck's broad—*hard, and so much of him*—chest. Containers flew from her arms, and she gave a small cry of dismay, quickly cut short when the jars were caught in midair by his hands—*large, and oh so manly hands. Hands I'd like to feel in more places than the small of my back. Stop it!*

"Easy, darlin'," he said, setting down the jars and reaching to pluck the rest of the items from her hands. "Where's the bread?" Settling in as if he had been in her kitchen a million times before, he unerringly opened the silverware drawer and pulled out a knife. Twisting his neck, he looked at her, one eyebrow lifted as his lips slowly curled into a—*sexy, oh God, is that grin ever sexy*—grin. "Vanna, the bread?"

The dance had thrown her off balance. The sweet, tender, incredibly beautiful dance. A dance she would hold close to her heart for years, because it wasn't like any experience she'd ever had before. So, it threw her terribly off balance, because he was a Rebel Wayfarer. She'd seen his patch. Well known to her, she recognized the emblem because Gunny was in the same club. She had been to Indiana several times over the past two years, meeting most of the local members as well as many from other chapters, but she'd never seen or heard of Truck. His bottom patch said 'Nomad,' but he held an officer's title. Confusing. Filled with a sudden urgency to know how this man fit into her friends' lives, she blurted, "Truck, you're a Rebel. Where's your bike?"

He set the knife down and turned to lean against the counter, standing close beside her. "Left it parked at the house"—gesturing to the south—"since it was a short walk from there to here." He lifted one shoulder and let it fall. "Saw there were lights on here when I went past. When I got there and saw the state of things, I hoped whoever lived here would still be up." That shoulder lifted again, the motion easy, he was comfortable in his body. "Bike's a little noisy, figured the wrong way to make a good first impression would be to wake the whole damn house when shoe leather would work just fine."

Ducking her chin, she kept her gaze directed to the floor so he wouldn't see the disappointment on her face when she moved away. "Lucky I'm a night owl," she murmured. *Not fate*, she thought, just a convenient neighbor.

Retrieving a loaf of bread from the box in the corner of the cabinet, she grabbed two plates from the shelf and a bag of chips from the snack drawer, moving back to stand beside him. Close, but not too close. Working in what she hoped was a companionable silence, they assembled sandwiches, one for her and two for him. Then, still wordless, she led him back to the living room where Christmas music was still softly playing.

Over the simple meal, Truck talked, telling her stories about all the places he'd been. He mentioned names, smiling at her when she nodded at him, indicating she knew at least some of the folks he spent time and shared history with. And she did know many of them, including Mason, Slate, Gunny, Hoss, Jase, and Deke. These men all seemed to be in his inner circle of confidantes, which didn't surprise her, because they were the elite in the club. But she was pleased to hear his experiences with them extended well beyond the organization itself, he also seemed to know their women and families. She watched as his face softened when he spoke of their children.

"I heard about the trouble Gunny's gal found herself in, how no one knew she was Jase's sister." He shook his head. "Glad of where she wound up, though. Woman's good for my brother, he needed her."

Vanna shook her head, "She needed him just as badly." Chuckling, she stirred the chips on her plate with one finger, looking down. "Sharon lived with me for a couple of years before she…healed enough to try things on her own again." She pinched the crust off one edge of her sandwich, tearing it into chunks and tossing them one at a time into her mouth. "I didn't find out until months later that I already knew Gunny."

Glancing up, she saw he was watching her avidly, listening with a peculiar focus to her words. "I knew him as 'Lost Lane.' Back before he met Deke, before the Rebels." She pushed back in her chair, lifting one leg to tuck her calf underneath her. "We met under…questionable circumstances, in the woods." She laughed. "But he quickly won me over with his impeccable good manners and dashing charm."

She told him about meeting Gunny, a name Lane was trying to outrun at the time, one fully embraced now. Backwoods Indiana, his appearance frightening, but her gut said his was a wounded soul, one she wanted to soothe. As she would hope someone would attempt to soothe her Kitt under the same circumstances.

It was Truck's turn to laugh and she watched his face change when he did, the wary look he had worn almost constantly since looking at her pictures fading away. The sound of his amusement filled the room and she smiled in response before saying, "What? I'm serious. He was…is a good man. Offered me coffee right away. Tried to set me at ease, which meant a lot." She sighed, thinking of those days spent hiking with Lane…Gunny. Listening to his shocking stories of war, and seeing firsthand the extent of what that horror could do to a person. In those days, he had been filled with fear, holding onto control with a loosely gathered fist. Gunny, the husband and father, was a different person, and every time she saw him she was even more proud of how he had grown and changed through the years.

In his first interactions she had seen echoes of her son's avoidance of touch, the unease if someone tried to hold his gaze too long. Gunny had shared himself little by little through the days as they hiked. Words coming easier with each mile passing underneath their feet, and now she treasured those memories above so much. Seeing him with her Sharon, how careful he was with Kitt, and his tenderness with the children he and Sharon had, she knew her instincts were true, she had been right to trust him.

Truck ate up her stories, his reactions urging her forward in her recitations. His laughter became something she sought to provoke, feeling as though each outburst was an earned reward. He gave himself fully to the emotion, something she suspected was a regular occurrence in his life. Something she found inordinately attractive, seeing it in contrast to her own necessarily regimented responses.

"How did you meet Sharon?" She had become so lost in the memories that his question surprised her, but she quickly recovered.

"I pulled her out of a ditch." She grinned at his skeptical look. "Literally. She was nose-deep in a canal in Florida, hiding from her then-husband. She had been beaten within an inch of her life, and still screwed up the courage to leave as soon as she saw an opening. Then she found the courage to trust the crazy woman standing on the lip of that ditch, hand held out." Shaking her head, she twisted and set her plate aside; suddenly realizing she hadn't brought in drinks for them. "I'm so sorry, I didn't even think about drinks. Would you like tea, or lemonade?" She thought a moment. "I might have a beer, but it'd be questionable whether you'd get skunky or not."

"Just water would be fine, Vanna." He shifted on the couch, stretching his legs with a suppressed groan. She pushed an ottoman towards him with one bare foot.

"Put your feet up if you like. Your boots can't hurt the footstool more than my boy has." His eyes filled with questions, immediately lifting to meet hers. She watched as his gaze cut to a picture of her standing next to Kitt, then back to her.

"Be right back," she said, ignoring those unspoken questions for now. *For now? That implies there's a later, woman.* Her inward scoff was thick with sarcasm and she winced a little. *He's nice, polite, good-looking, a great dancer, eloquent, a good listener, likes vinyl, and rides a motorcycle. Of course there won't be a later. Man like him? Taken. Always. He simply hasn't mentioned his woman's name yet.* She stood in the kitchen for a minute, then another, waiting on the flush in her cheeks to subside, the empty ache from earlier in the evening again settling in her chest.

"He's the new neighbor, and we happen to know people in common. Be nice, Savannah." *He'll finish eating and then be gone...and why does that thought make me wanna cry?*

Back in the living room, she was reaching out to place a bottle of water on a coaster next to his plate when his hand captured hers, holding her in place. "Vanna, relax, honey. If I'm making you nervous, I can go. I've been here for hours, darlin'." He gestured to his plate, "You've fed me, entertained me. Kept me company. Interested me, way more than you know. Made me feel more at home than I've felt for years. You've been more than hospitable, and while I've enjoyed our conversation and time together immensely, it would be a poor return if I overstayed my welcome. You say the word, darlin', I'm outta your hair."

"No, Truck. You're fine. I've had a wonderful evening as well. Glad I was still awake and able to help out." Tugging her hand loose, she stepped back, nearly tripping over the ottoman. "Since we're new neighbors and all."

His eyes flared, gaze trapping her for a moment and then in a flat tone slowly said, "Yeah, new neighbors."

She had barely regained her seat when footsteps sounded overhead. A groan escaped her throat before she could suppress it. *Crap, Kitt's up.* She whipped her head sideways to see it was nearly three o'clock in the morning—*we've been talking for four hours?*—then whipped just as fast the other direction, grimacing at the still uneaten cookies plated next to the half-glass of milk. Normally nibbling on the cookies was the last thing she did before heading to bed on Christmas Eve, helping feed Kitt's belief for another year, but she hadn't gotten to bed yet tonight. Now, Kitt was up and she knew he would be on a mission to see if Santa had come. *Crap*.

"Hand them to me." The order was spoken in a low tone, similar to the do-not-ignore-me voice she used with Kitt, and got the same instant reaction from her that it would from Kitt. Barely a second passed before she scooped up the plate and glass, passing them to Truck without argument.

Kitt's footsteps slowed when he hit the stairs, probably confused by the number of lights still brightly shining on the main floor. "Mom?" The voice sounded more than a little frightened, and the question in the form of her name repeated before she could respond. "Mom?"

"Here, honey," she called, and then told him, "I'm not alone. It's okay. I have a friend in the living room with me." It wouldn't do for him to be startled at seeing a stranger in their house in the middle of the night. He would still be startled, but at least he had some advance warning this way. "I'm in here."

Standing between Truck and the entryway, she looked over her shoulder at where he was seated on the couch. Her glance just in time to see him place three pieces of cookie back on the plate, a large bite taken from each one. As she watched he upended the glass of milk which she knew had to be warm by now, chugging down a little more than half. Then he reached out and put the glass and plate on the table next to where he sat, smiling up at her. "You've got a little," she motioned to her upper lip and his smile changed to a broad grin as he reached up to wipe the milk from his mustache. "Got it," she whispered, turning back to see Kitt standing in the dining room, looking past her at Truck with an expression she couldn't place.

"MOM!" His shout was loud and both hands lifted shoulder high, elbows bent, tucked tight to his side. "VANNA MOM!" He danced from foot to foot, mouth open in a huge 'O', hands flapping madly in the air. This could be either extreme excitement...or fear.

"Right here, honey. I'm right here." Unsure of what his reaction meant, she stayed focused on him even when the shadows moving in the room indicated Truck had climbed to his feet. Kitt's gaze tracked up and up over her shoulder, and then his face split in half in what was absolutely the widest smile she had ever seen from him.

"SANTA!"

"Oh, shit," Truck muttered, and her thoughts echoed his words.

Oh, crap.

Chapter Five

Truck

Vanna's son shouted again, this time wordless, and launched himself around her and at Truck. Bracing, because while the kid was clearly all boy, he was still as big as a man. Truck's arms closed around Kitt when he hit Truck's chest, holding them both upright with some effort. "SANTA!" Shouting into his shoulder, the boy was bouncing up and down in place, jolting him with every jump. "MOM! SANTA!"

"Honey," Vanna's voice sounded strained and Truck lifted his head to see her eyes were fixed on her son's back. "Kitt…" Trailing off, her voice was soft, but still strained and he saw she had rolled her lips between her teeth, biting down hard. Lifting her chin, she reached out one arm, hand hovering just over the boy's shoulder as she said, "Kitt, I need you to let the man go."

"SANTA!" Head shaking back and forth vigorously, Kitt, because surely that was the boy's name, loudly refused. "NO!" His arms tightened around Truck's chest and squeezed hard, then relaxed a little when Truck didn't release him or push away. Softly, quietly, Kitt sighed, "Santa came."

Truck caught Vanna's eyes and smiled, hoping she would understand what he was about to do. From her reaction it was obvious her son was...different. Her caution in touching him shouted how out of character it must be for the boy to have wrapped himself around a stranger. Kitt's vocabulary seemed limited, but she wasn't restricting herself to baby talk, so Truck assumed Kitt understood more than he said.

Squeezing Kitt gently, he said, "Of course I came. I always take care of the good boys." Kitt's jumps had slowed, but at Truck's words they turned back into bounds, the boy's shoulder catching him under the chin with every other jarring hop. "But, good boys don't get their presents in the middle of the night. Good boys wait until morning, when their mothers say it's okay to be up and about." The hops stopped abruptly and he saw Vanna's face pale. "I think you're a good boy, Kitt. Are you a good boy?"

Head nodding fast, Kitt still held on, fists pressed into Truck's back, fingers clutching the shirt underneath his cut. "Santa."

"Yes, Kitt?" Arms slowly relaxing, he leaned back, looking down as Kitt moved slightly away.

"I good." Eyes darting back and forth across Truck's face, Kitt came to a decision. "Santa good."

"Yes, honey," Vanna crooned, "Santa knows you're a good boy. Let's get you back upstairs and tucked in. It's been a busy few days, no wonder you are up early. Everything all thrown off track." Her palm landed between Kitt's shoulder blades and she stroked slowly up and down. The steady, even pressure of her caress transferring to Truck through the boy's body as he melted at his mother's touch. Kitt liked the feel of that, and even liking it, Truck suspected the boy didn't often allow it.

"No, stay Santa. Want stay Santa." Kitt's grip tightened again but Vanna's soothing touch never faltered.

"Santa has lots of other houses to visit, honey. He was just finishing up here. He's gonna have to head out." She edged closer, reaching out to balance herself with a hand on Truck's bicep. "Just finishing up, so you can have Christmas in the morning. In the morning, honey. Not right now. You want to have Christmas in the morning, right? So do the other good boys and girls, so Santa's gonna have to travel to their houses, too."

"Santa go?" The kid sounded heartbroken and he burrowed his face into Truck's shoulder, resting his forehead there for a moment. "Santa go." This wasn't a question, but an acceptance of the inevitable and Truck's mouth got tight at the sadness echoing through the boy. Then Kitt turned acceptance into a demand. "Like Santa. No go. Santa no go."

"Santa likes you, too, Kitt," Truck said immediately and Kitt stood straighter, tipping his chin up to look at Truck's face. "Santa likes you a lot, kiddo."

Tilting his head to one side, Kitt dipped an ear to his shoulder as he looked at Truck's vest. "That not say Santa." He was focused on the name patch stitched to the right-hand lapel of the vest, and Truck grinned. "Santa?"

"Yeah, Kitt?"

"Not Santa?" Kitt lifted a hand and tugged gently on Truck's beard, pulling a laugh from him.

"Beard's kinda attached, kiddo." He pointed at the patch. "That's my nickname. Truck." Grinning at Vanna over Kitt's shoulder, he was glad to see her smile in return. "People call me Truck so they don't give away my real identity. It's a secret. Can you keep my secret, and call me Truck?"

Eyes narrowed, Kitt considered this for a minute, then grinned and nodded. "Two door, three door, four door, crew cab," tipping his chin up further, he stared at the ceiling, continuing his confusing recitation of words. "Dually, dual axle, fifth wheel." Pausing he sighed, rolling his eyes at whatever it was the ceiling wasn't telling him. "Flatbed, dump, stepside, fleetside, cargo." He sighed again, stepping back and turning to look at his mother. "Truck Santa."

"Yeah, honey. This is Truck. He's a friend, but has to go, and it's time for you to head back to bed." Vanna was clearly accustomed to dealing with Kitt and his behaviors, and she gently urged him towards the stairs. Kitt was halfway there when he spun and ran back to stand in front of Truck.

"Four, six, eight, V, inline. Automatic, standard, three speed, four speed, five speed, overdrive, four wheel." Kitt sucked in a breath and on the outward burst of air said, "Truck."

Truck bent his knees slightly, dipping down to look into Kitt's face. "Head back up to bed now, Kitt. Merry Christmas, son."

Eyes bright, Kitt whispered the words back to him, "Merry Christmas." Dropping his gaze, he was staring somewhere in the vicinity of the second button on Truck's shirt when he said, "Leave the ornaments.

Ornaments stay on the tree until two days past when Santa comes. Santa came. Merry Christmas."

"Right-o, will do, son." He smiled and held still as Kitt reached out, wrapping one arm around his chest to pull close in an awkward hug. "Goodnight, Kitt."

"Ni-night."

Palm resting on Kitt's back, Vanna twisted her neck to look over her shoulder at Truck, mouthing the words, "I'll be back." He nodded and sat down on the couch, slowly reaching out for the plate with the half-finished cookies. As he ate, without her there he was free to look around her living room, taking in the comfortable but uncluttered décor with a different eye. No sign of a man anywhere, this was a carefully neutral room not coming close to reflecting the personality of the owner, much less a spouse or significant other. *No old man here*, he thought.

Twisting to look at the rest of the pictures, he saw evidence that even when she was with a group, if she wasn't with Kitt, she was alone. Friendly, the pictures attested to that, but even with friends she stood by herself for the most part. Woman alone on Christmas Eve, opening her home to a stranger, offering to break bread with him. That made him think her being alone wasn't a decision so much as something thrust on her. Alone, and maybe lonely. She had rushed to accept his conversational openers, showing him her interest without guile. Taking it farther, trusting him with her memories and stories, and trusting him to be careful with her son. Warm and giving, Vanna was so much more than her house might make a person think.

He remembered the precise placement of things in the kitchen, making it easy for him to track where things would be. He would bet money that her entire house was arranged for Kitt. Arranged and decorated with the boy's needs in mind.

"What a good momma," he whispered, setting the empty plate on the table, stacking the plates together. He grinned at the memory of her panicked look when she realized her son was on his way downstairs and all evidence pointed to Santa having bypassed their house that night. A few bites of sweet cookie and a quick storytime for a boy was small repayment for the hospitality she'd offered him tonight. "Do it again, anytime."

He stroked his beard slowly, shaking his head. Wasn't the first time kids had mistaken him for Santa, and sometimes he even dressed the part at the club's holiday parties. Toting around a big red bag, handing out brightly wrapped presents to the kiddos, heart hurting that none of them were his. Leaning his head back against the couch cushions, he finally pieced together all the things Kitt had said there at the end, realizing they were different kinds and types of trucks. "Truck Santa." He laughed quietly, eyes sinking closed.

Chapter Six

Vanna

She stood in the archway between the living and dining rooms, listening to the soft skritching crackle of the record player battling the quiet breathing coming from the couch. It had taken longer than expected to calm Kitt and get him back to sleep. She had perched on the edge of a chair in his room for a long time, waiting until he settled in and finally dozed off.

Down here it looked like Truck had done the same. His boots lined up near one arm of the couch. Him on his back, body stretched along the length of the cushioned seat. Leather vest still on, he had his arms crossed tightly across his chest, and looked cold.

She grabbed a blanket from a stack on a nearby chair. Stretching her arms out she softly flipped it once, letting it float and land on top of the man sleeping on her couch. She had just leaned in to tug it higher on his shoulders when he opened his amazing blue eyes and stared up at her, blinking sleepily. With a groan, he wrapped one palm around her wrist and tugged, pulling her down on top of him. Shifting and turning, he rolled them so she was wedged between his body and the back of the couch, then snaked his arms around her, shoving one arm underneath her so he could wrap her up tightly.

"Truck," she called softly and he grunted in response, lifting his chin to place his lips on her forehead. "Truck, you fell asleep."

"And, I'll stay that way, you quit talkin', Vanna." His words proved he knew exactly where he was, and his next ones shocked her into silence. His lips moved against her skin as he said, "He's a good kid, woman. Means he's got a good momma. I like good people, know 'em when I see 'em. I see a good person in you, Vanna. I don't know about you, but I could use some sleep, and I could use someone to hold for a change while I do it."

Silence fell around them, but it wasn't uncomfortable. This was an easy quiet, companionable, filled with the presence of another person, but in a way that was perfectly...right. She felt the difference when he slipped back into sleep, his arms were heavier, his breathing deeper and slower. Relaxed, comfortable, her silence and acceptance of his embrace gifting him with oblivion.

About ten minutes later, she received the same gift in return.

SECRET SANTA

Chapter Seven

Truck

He stretched and rolled, pushing up to sit on the edge of the couch, twisting to look back at the woman he'd left still sleeping. Face buried in a throw pillow, Vanna sighed and shifted, hand slipping out palm-down, seeking. Strands of unruly hair had escaped her severe hairstyle and he reached out, using the tip of one finger to tuck it behind her ear. *Beauty queen*, he remembered his first thoughts upon seeing her last night, finding them still agreeable. But, after only a few hours he felt he knew her to be so much more than that.

Mother: sweet and patient, kind and loving.

Snuggler: stealer of covers, under-chin burrower.

Linguist: conversationalist extraordinaire, witty story spinner.

Dancer: talented, rhythmic, sexy swayer.

What if she's what you've been looking for? He asked himself the question he had so often posed to his brothers over the years, when they started weighing the pros and cons of taking an old lady. *Old lady? Getting a little ahead of yourself, aren't you, old man? You don't even know her last name.*

Kitt was stirring around upstairs; the sounds from the bathroom up there had woken Truck a few minutes ago. Rising to his feet he went to the kitchen and opened the cabinet to see three boxes of cereal, all the same kind. With a grin he found spoons and grabbed two bowls, pulling them down from an identical stack, and poured some of the healthy multi-grain into each, finding the sugar and spooning a couple of heaps into what he now considered 'his' bowl. Kitt wandered into the kitchen, eyes barely open until he saw Truck. Before he could shout his excitement, Truck put out a hand, palm down, patting the air in a 'keep it quiet' motion. "Hey, Kitt. Mornin'. Your mom's still sleepin'. Let's let her sleep in a bit, yeah?"

With a slow nod Kitt pressed his lips together tightly and without questioning Truck's presence went to the bowls. He picked up one of the spoons from the counter and silently looked down, then up at Truck. "Milk, I know. I gotcha." Topping both up with milk until the circles of cereal floated, he picked his up and stood, leaning against the countertop next to Kitt as they spooned up cereal for breakfast. "You sleep okay, Kitt?"

Head nodding loosely on his bent neck, Kitt paused eating long enough to grunt what must have been agreement. He finished his cereal and stood, cutting his eyes towards Truck's bowl, still cradled in his hand.

Truck grinned, tipping it to his lips and drank the remaining milk down before setting it on the counter. It had no sooner come into contact with the surface before Kitt grabbed it, moving to the sink.

Lip caught between his teeth, Kitt spread a cloth on the sink divider, then squirted liquid soap on the fabric. Carefully twisting the water faucet, he dripped water onto the cloth, wetting it, then worked it to a lather. He used it to swipe the bowls and spoons. Setting the dishes down Kitt reached towards the lever controlling the water, then drew his hand back. He huffed out a breath and reached out again, a grimace twisting his features. Bumping the lever with the back of his hand, he stood and stared at the resulting water flow for a time. Seconds ticking up into a minute, then two, Kitt was frozen in place as the water ran down the sink.

"Kitt," Truck called, shuffling closer. "Want me to finish up with that?"

Head shaking fiercely back and forth, Kitt grunted, his shoulders and chest rising and falling with the effort. As he reached out towards the sink Truck saw the boy's hands were shaking, trembling as if he were freezing in a deep, cold snow.

"Son," he called, concerned because Kitt seemed to be working up to something that was either painful, or scared the shit out of him. "Let me help you."

"NO!" With his first word of the morning, Kitt exploded, slapping at the lip of the counter where it edged the sinks. "NO!" Knuckles cracking against the hard surface, he emphasized his frustration with deep rhythmic grunting.

Shit, Truck thought, *this ain't good*. Without giving himself time to think he reached out and turned off the water, not surprised when Kitt immediately subsided. Holding out his hand, he offered, "Let's do it together," shocked and surprised when Kitt's hand rose to grip his. "We don't need much water to do this little bit of dishes." Fingers to the lever, ready to turn the water off again if needed, Truck tipped it slowly, allowing only the smallest of flows out the faucet. "Don't even need to get our hands wet if we don't want to." Stretching his arm out, he moved their clasped hands towards the bowls, shoving first one dish then the other underneath the water, drawing back as the bowls collected water.

Finger and thumb clasped the spoons and Truck let them fall, one at a time, clattering into one of the bowls. "We don't even have to touch the water."

"Water okay." He turned to look at Kitt to see the boy had twisted away, staring out the kitchen window at the creek running alongside the trees across the field. "Water," Kitt sighed, lifting his other hand to scrub at his forehead. "Running." A shudder rippled through him and his gaze cut back to the slowly flowing water coming from the faucet. On a long exhale, he breathed out the word. "Bad."

"Well, we have plenty of water now. We can turn this sucker off anytime," Truck said, bringing their hands up to tip the faucet off and the tension in Kitt's hand and arm immediately dissolved, leaving him loose and compliant. "You mind if I help you finish up with the dishes? Would that be okay, Kitt?"

"Yes," Kitt said, fingers tightening around Truck's hand again. This time the boy led the way, bringing their hands towards the water-filled bowls fearlessly, fingers dipping into the surface to retrieve the spoons. More carefully he tipped the bowls sideways, relieving them of their burdens, watching with a shiver as the water flowed away down the drain.

"Did I miss breakfast?"

Vanna's voice came from behind them, startling a happy, "MOM!" from Kitt who turned, still holding

Truck's hand, pulling him around. "SANTA!" Kitt shouted this, then his voice dropped to a whisper as he excitedly hissed, "*Secret* Santa. *Truck*."

Kitt's arm shot skywards, dragging Truck's with it as he shouted, "PRESENTS!" Dashing across the kitchen towards his mother, he pulled Truck along in his wake, their hands still clasped tightly together. As he pushed past his mother, he grabbed her hand with his other one, dragging her across the room towards the still-lighted Christmas tree. "PRESENTS!"

Dropping their hands, he grabbed up an old, tattered Santa hat from underneath the tree and turned, lifting it. Rising on his toes, Kitt placed it on top of Truck's hair, tugging it gently down into place over his ponytail. "Santa," Kitt whispered, his eyes meeting Truck's for a second before he looked away. "Vanna Mom's Santa."

Legs collapsing under him, Kitt settled to the floor next to the tree, chin tipped up and gaze flickering back and forth between Truck and Vanna. "My Santa."

Chapter Eight

Vanna

Jesus, she thought, *how did I get to this place on Christmas morning, where my son is washing dishes with the man who chastely slept with me on the couch last night?* Chin down, she was smiling at Kitt's antics as he shifted presents around underneath the tree and hadn't seen Truck moving closer. "He's excited." His voice at her ear surprised her so she twisted her neck, turning towards him, shocked when he brushed his lips across hers. "Mornin', darlin'."

Without another word he folded his legs, positioning himself near Kitt, the two male faces looking up at her with similar expectant expressions. Truck added a hand lifted her direction, palm out invitingly. He waited patiently until she wrapped her fingers around his, using the support as she lowered herself to the floor, too.

"Time for presents, Kitt," Truck said with a grin. "You've been a good boy. The best. Waited until your momma was ready. Time for your reward, son."

Bright-eyed, Kitt twisted and dug under the tree, focused as he began to sort the presents. Vanna knew from past Christmases he would have two piles at the end of this exercise, one for her and one for him. Truck's hand gave hers a squeeze and she looked at him, surprised to realize he had drawn her hand to his lap, cradling it with both of his. "He's a good boy," he told her softly, startling a laugh from her. At the sound his expression gentled, growing tender as he looked at her. "Seems to have a real good momma."

"Thanks," she said. *He's all I have.* "He's my best boy. Keeps me on my toes, that's for sure." She knew her smile had faded when his did as well, and she tried to toss off the melancholy with a quick acknowledgement. "Thank you for your patience with him this morning. You hit just the right tone."

"How old was he when he was diagnosed?" Truck surprised her by going straight to the heart of things, indicating his reactions to Kitt's behavior might be grounded in a personal knowledge tied to a natural caring soul.

"Not until he was older. Nearly six." She shook her head, twisting to look away from Truck's too-knowing gaze, taking in Kitt's antics instead. "I knew at three that something wasn't right." She shook her head. "I'm not a fan of labels, but I have a slew of them if you need one. Just not right here," she hesitated, cutting a glance back to Truck, seeing his eyes trained steadily on her, "not right now. Let me have Christmas."

"You got it," Truck immediately told her, his reassuring words nearly lost as Kitt chose that same moment to hoot in delight. He had the presents placed on either side of his legs, packages lined up from smallest to largest. Her side had three boxes, his held more than a dozen.

"Ready?" She asked Kitt the beginning question, saw him starting to squirm in place in anticipation. "Set?" The second question normally settled him to stillness, waiting for the release of the final word in their present-opening traditional game. This time however, he threw up one hand in a clear 'halt' signal. She rocked back on her bottom, and then bent her knees so she could lean farther forward. "What, Kitt?"

His eyes were working their way along the boxes, paper and bows individual to each package, name tags held in place with curling ribbons. Hers marked with a 'V' or an 'M,' depending on the gift's origin, and Kitt knew those were hers. His presents all had his name on them, unmistakable and easy to differentiate from hers. "What's wrong, honey?"

Features twisted, he was thinking hard about something, and she didn't have any clues to help determine where he was headed. He shifted, rocking hip-to-hip, making more room for himself, the expression on his face fiercely intense as he looked up at Truck. "Wait," he whispered. Thrusting to his feet, he sidestepped where she and Truck sat side-by-side, calling over his shoulder as he ran out of the room, "Wait."

"What's he doing?" Truck asked, and she shook her head, hearing Kitt's feet pound up the stairs. He ran to his room and stomped around and around as she listened to him muttering to himself, his voice rising and falling in frustration.

"No idea. Sometimes it's just better to go with the flow." She tipped her chin down, not wanting to meet his gaze. Gratitude was hard for her to express. "Look, Truck, I appreciate your help with him last night. That could have derailed his whole night. You were awesome."

He sighed and moved away slightly, saying, "But…" drawing out the one word.

She looked up at him, seeing his face had drawn into hard lines. "But?"

"Yeah, I hear it coming. It's the 'Thanks, but,' speech. I'm just saving you the trouble of finishing it." He released her hand and climbed to one knee, looking down at her. "Kitt told me to wait, but I think it's time for me to head out." He grabbed his boots, sliding them on and tucking the loose laces inside with angry movements. "I see I managed to overstay my welcome after all."

Two seconds later, he was out the door and gone.

Chapter Nine

Truck

"Shit." He tipped his head back, looking at the tops of the trees as they swayed against the sky. Their sensuous movements reminding him of how Vanna felt in his arms last night, dancing with him across her living room. Bending over, he stared at the ground as he laced up his boots, slapping the leather into the hooks by rote. *Beautiful woman like that; inside even more beauty than what she carries on her outside. No way she'd want someone like me around her and her kid.*

"Take what you can get," he muttered, calling up the memories of how it felt to have her resting against him on the couch. Waking up to the scent of her hair. The little noises she made when he pulled away, how she reached for him in her sleep. "I'll take it. Sweet. Beautiful." The softness of her lips when he kissed her in front of the Christmas tree and her excited man-boy. *I nearly forgot who she is*, he thought, remembering the pictures on her wall. *Who I am.* He saw the clubhouse in Little Rock in his head, long bar stretching out, stools inhabited only by men like him, lonely ones without family. *Glad she cut the ribbons quick, before anything tied us together.*

Leticia's voice slipped through his head, sounding somehow fainter than the last time she spoke when she said, *You're selling yourself short, my love.*

His steps faltered and slowed as his thumb absently rubbed across his lips, feeling the ghost of a touch there. He hadn't imagined Leticia for months now. *It's time for you to find someone you can let in, Peter. She's a perfect fit for you. I see good things.*

"You saw good things everywhere you looked, Tish." He had stopped walking, a breathing statue in the little woods between Vanna's house and the one he had purchased sight-unseen from an old friend.

Only because there were good things to be seen. You. Our friends. Our life. Does it surprise you I still see good things? Like the possibility of a new life for you, one that doesn't come with loneliness as its only companion? Her voice was inside his head and he didn't even have to answer her, he knew she'd heard his rejection of the idea when she laughed, the sound as light and easy as moonlight on a field. *Peter, I want to see you happy again. Can't you get that through your thick skull? I want that for you, want you to feel alive, feel love. To feel treasured. That woman needs something to treasure, why would you want to deny her that?*

Leticia had been his girlfriend, once upon a time. Theirs hadn't been a fantastical love story, made up of incredible coincidences and circumstance, but a normal boy-meets-girl moment in a bar that led to a night of satisfaction, which in turn led to what should have been a lifetime of the same. "I loved you." *I know you did. You do, or you wouldn't be doing this to yourself.*

Her death had been sudden. Shocking in its swiftness. Two years they'd been together, a year of her living with him. Working long hours, she wore herself out and caught a cold. She had a stupid common cold, went to bed feeling like crap, and never woke up. Nearly twenty years ago, he had gone in to wake her for supper to find her cold and still, resting peacefully, head on the pillow and covers pulled to her chin.

Her death was what led him to the life of a wandering outlaw and eventually brought him to the Rebels. He counted himself lucky that he had found a club like them on his first go-around. "I miss you." *I know you do. There's a hole in you that needs filling,*

Peter. See if this woman can help fill it. Right now, she needs you more than ever.

With a sigh, he shook off the stillness that had settled on him and started his legs moving, striding forward and away from Vanna. Tromping through the woods, he was muttering to himself about fools and their feelings when he heard shouting coming from behind him.

The shouting came again, and he recognized Vanna's voice, fear threading through him as he heard her yell, the words terrifyingly clear. "Kitt, where are you?"

Anxiety jolted in his chest, squeezing his heart, and without hesitation he turned and ran back the way he'd come. Through the trees and towards the sound of her voice. His long legs ate up the distance as he dodged around trunks and jumped over deadfalls. *Kitt*, he thought, skirting a tree to see a path crossing from left to right in front of him and he quickly veered to run along this open space. *What the hell did you do, boy?*

Vanna's shout was much closer when it came a second time, and as he rounded the next muddy corner he saw her standing in the middle of the path. Still in her pajamas, her feet bare, she looked frantic. Hands cupped around her mouth, she was swinging in a circle, her eyes wide and frightened, calling for her son. "Kitt! Where are you?"

Within a heartbeat, he had reached her and gripped her shoulders, turning her to face him. He was about to give her a little shake when her face began to crumple, eyes clenching tightly shut, lips pressed painfully together. Instead of shaking her he wrapped his arms around her, pulling her against his chest. "Darlin', talk to me." He dropped his chin, mouth beside her ear, firmly urging her, "Tell me what happened."

"He-he-he ran out-out of the ha-house." Voice hitching, her shaking words were hardly loud enough for him to hear. "He was so ma-mad." Shoulders shaking, she sucked in a hard breath and he squeezed her.

"Slow down, Vanna. Take a breath, darlin'. Talk to me."

"He gets mad like that sometimes, but he's never run away like this." Pushing against his chest, she fought for room between them and leaned back, looking up at him with tears streaking her cheeks. Her voice dropped to a whisper when she repeated, "He was *so* mad."

"Where would he go?" Even as he asked the question she was shaking her head.

"I don't know. He's never done this before." Tipping her chin, she rested her forehead against his chest, desperation flowing through her voice. "I don't *know*."

"Easy, darlin'. Think. Did you check your car? The garage?" Without lifting her head she shook it back and forth, weight pressing against him as she moved.

"I ran out right behind him but he was already gone." The deep breath seemed to come easier this time, and she blew it back out slowly. He stroked one hand rhythmically up and down her back, caressing and calming her as she had with Kitt last night, and he felt her sag into him. He knew she'd locked down her emotions and had self-control again when she said decisively, "The creek. His favorite place here in the woods is the creek."

"Take me there," he ordered, stepping back and bending slightly, arms out.

He'd intended to scoop her up, but she took his movement as part of his spoken order and twisted out of his grip. Running up the path, she called over her shoulder, "It's not far."

Pelting up the path behind her, he watched the soles of her bare feet as she ran ahead of him, the pale flesh darkening with each contact against the earth, hints of red mixing with the dirt. "Is it deep?" He yelled the question, fighting against himself to stay behind her. Fighting the instinct to move his size fifteens and run ahead even without knowing the way. "The creek, is it deep?"

Without slowing she called back, "In places, yes."

His next question forced out of him by fear, he shouted, "Can Kitt swim?"

Her neck twisted, head turning to cut a terrified glance back at him and he knew exactly why she was running as fast as she could. "No."

SECRET SANTA

Chapter Ten

Kitt

The water swirled around the edges of the rocks and branches Vanna Mom had used to extend the pool of water, building a barrier the water had to work to get around. That made it stay longer in one place, and Vanna Mom said it didn't hurt the creek to wait a little while before it left them. This notch in the creek bank had been created one spring in a flood. Blocked by a downed tree, the rushing water had carved out a broad circle before it ran in a wall down the creek, taking the bridge with it, breaking the road where the creek flowed through. "Creek, stream, waterway, river, crick."

Vanna Mom said the pool was deep on one side. She stayed in the shallows when she looked to find his treasures. Shiny, flat rocks, smoothed by giant's feet. Wiggling tadpoles, sometimes with frog feet poking out on either side of their tadpole tail. Possible frogs, Vanna Mom called them. Pinching crawdads, dragged from their safe, blind burrows in the mud to the bright light of day, their actions as confused as his brain felt most days. "Crawdad, crawfish, crayfish, mudbug."

He took a step forward, looking around. This was the only place he wanted to be after he came downstairs to see Truck hadn't waited. And Vanna Mom was sad because Truck was a treasure. So sad Kitt couldn't stand to be there, her sad beat in on him from all sides and he wanted her not sad.

This was a good place, one where he saw happy faces. Where Vanna Mom found so many treasures. He'd lost count of the things saved, as well as the treasures gently transferred back to the water. Hands clutching the hastily wrapped present against his chest, he tightened his grip on the rectangle, the edges of the unsecured paper fluttering in the breeze. *I wanted to find her a treasure*, he thought.

Another step forward, looking around again, nearly on top of the rushing water. "Scary water. Fast water."

The bank crumbled underfoot and he fell, his cry of fear cut short when the water closed over his head.

Chapter Eleven
Truck

He heard Kitt's shout over the noise of running water. Heard it stop. Truck exploded through the bushes and into a small clearing right behind Vanna, to see...nothing. The sound of water came from directly ahead, but he couldn't see the creek. Couldn't see Kitt. Couldn't hear him, either. Truck's steps faltered and Vanna flew ahead. Then he saw it, recognized the dip across the field that hid the waterway, meandering alongside the edge of the clearing where it butted up against the woods. Head down, he put on speed and passed her, a dozen strides later brought him to the edge of the bank to see a fresh scar where the edge had given way.

Without a thought for his own safety, he launched himself off the bank and into the water, bones jarring in his body when his boots unexpectedly met the gravel of a solid but shallow sandbar. Laughter came from behind him and he turned, twisting in the calf-deep water to see Kitt lying just below the bank. Mud smeared on his face, the boy was flat on his back in about ten-inches of water. Kitt was holding onto something with one hand, the soggy wrapping paper losing its glitter as the gently flowing water tugged at the edges. He was gleefully slapping at the water with his other hand, splashing and making waves.

A shadow cut across Kitt's form and Truck looked up to see Vanna teetering on the edge. She held her balance for a moment, then stumbled as the bank let go again and she fell towards the water. With a lunge, he caught her in mid-air, arms wrapped around her back, her feet swinging and hitting his knees with the force of her arrested fall.

Still laughing, Kitt pointed at Truck where he stood in the middle of the creek holding his mother, and said, "Truck came."

Truck held her for a moment, savoring the feel of her even in this situation, before he let her slide down his front. By then she was fighting to get free, pushing and twisting in his arms. She let out a single shocked hiss when her bare feet hit the freezing water, and then she was gone. Turning away, high-stepping it through the waterway, she slipped on moss-covered rocks covering the creek bed. Truck moved with her, hands hovering to catch her again if needed. Stumbling backwards, she nearly took a tumble twice before collapsing on her knees beside Kitt.

The depth of her understanding of how the boy's head worked was proven when she reached him. There were no angry shouts from her, no furiously terrified threats to confuse Kitt. Instead she carefully gathered her son in her arms and Truck heard her say, "Brave boy. My Kitt's such a brave boy. Look at you, all covered in creek water. Sitting right here in the water, the biggest treasure I ever found. Look at you, my boy. My Kitt. How brave you are."

"Water," Kitt said and shrugged, struggling to sit up without losing his mother's touch. He held out the tattered thing he had been cradling to his chest. His gaze was stuck on the surface of the water, but the top of his head angled towards Truck. "Present."

"I see you have something for Truck," Vanna said. She shifted beside Kitt, and finally lost her battle to retain her feet, slippery rocks and swiftly-flowing water winning the day as they conspired to knock her on her ass. Her teeth had begun to chatter when she asked, "Can we go home first, Kitt?"

Kitt's gaze lifted from where it had been focused on watching the water flow around his legs and he looked at his mother. Drawing the package back to his chest, he reached out with his other hand, tapping two fingers against Vanna's shoulder, he said, "Treasure."

"Yes, Kitt. We'll come back and find treasures again, when the water's not quite so cold." Truck heard the tremble in her voice and knew it to be a combination of things. Relief at her boy safely found; the draining adrenaline drop following their successful rushing chase; and the December chill of the water seeping into her flesh. It was that last one he was most concerned with. Not only was she barefooted, the t-shirt and shin-length pajama bottoms she wore were thin and— soaked as they were—would offer no protection from the cold-for-Florida December day.

"NO!" Kitt shouted and his gaze lifted to Truck. "Truck's treasure." His hand thumped Vanna's shoulder again as his gaze dipped. "Home."

Chapter Twelve

Kitt

Truck helped Vanna Mom up the bank and away from the fast water. *Not scary. Not now.* Kitt scrambled up behind them, gripping roots one-handed, toes digging for purchase in the moving dirt. He laughed aloud when the hands lifted under his bottom and pushed, laughed louder when he heard the woman say, *Such a big boy*.

Vanna Mom stood beside Truck and Kitt moved to them, looking down to see Vanna Mom's toes curling up and away from the mud, while Kitt's toes dug down in, and Truck's boots stood on the surface. "Different," he said, and agreed when he heard, *Different isn't always bad*. "Up, down, on."

"Kitt," Truck said and Kitt tipped the top of his head to indicate he heard. "You okay to walk home, son?"

"Walk, pace, hike, stride, skip, hop." He could do any of those today. He could do all of them. He'd do better if he had shoes on, but he could walk home. *I know you can, Kitt*. "Can, could, would, should."

"Okay, let's get your momma home." Truck bent and picked up Vanna Mom, ignoring her protests that quivered in the air, making her sound like a bowl of jelly looked. She clattered like their dishes behind the little doors in the kitchen did when the trucks drove up and down their road, back before the water claimed the bridge. Kitt glanced up, saw her hands were folded in her lap, fingers grub-white and holding on tight to the ones next to them. Packed as tight as people in a church. "Here is the church, and this is the steeple." *Let's go home, Kitt*. "Home, house, building, residence, structure."

He turned to walk up the path, trying to match Truck's pace, his legs stretching far to make up in extension what he lacked in length. Truck laughed and Kitt sighed to hear the woman's laugh, too. "Maybe you could walk a bit faster, son?" *Walk, pace, hike*. He could hike. He hiked with Vanna Mom a lot; he could hike, even without boots. He hiked up the path and heard Truck say, "Good job, son."

MariaLisa deMora

Chapter Thirteen

Vanna

So cold, she thought. Eyes closed, she leaned against Truck's chest, feeling the swaying jostle of his every boot fall to the path winding through the woods. Kitt's footsteps preceding them, his bare soles slapping against the mud and dirt leading them home.

Her terror when he bolted from the house had been nearly paralyzing. He had always been a wanderer, but not a runner. She didn't anticipate his actions like she would have if it had been a common occurrence. But it wasn't. *I could have scripted it, otherwise.*

Thank God, Truck hadn't gotten far and heard her screams. Otherwise she might still be roving the paths through the woods, not thinking, just reacting. And Kitt would be lying in the water, cold and still. She shivered at the thought and Truck's arms tightened around her, his voice murmuring, "Nearly there, darlin'."

I really, really like it when he calls me that, she thought and allowed her head to tip sideways, pressing her cheek against his chest. There was something she wanted to tell him, but after he jumped to the wrong conclusion this morning, it probably wouldn't have mattered anyway. *What I'd like to tell him is* "You got it wrong, Truck."

"What'd I get wrong, darlin'?" In her imagination, his voice deepened, gained an edge of roughness.

"This morning. I wasn't kicking you out. I liked having you there. You got it wrong." The racking shudders had finally fled her bones, but they took all her remaining heat along with them. "That hurt." Everything hurt, and her skin felt as if she had spent too many hours exposed on a mountaintop, sun-raised blisters flaring painful heat all along the surface of her skin. "Freezing burns, I did not know that." *Even the words in my head are slurring now*, she thought, "I wanted you to stay. I danced with you. You *saw* me."

Her head tipped back against his arm and she looked up, holding her eyes open with effort in order to see his strong neck and that beautiful, full beard. "I just wanted to explain about Kitt."

"Hold on, darlin'. Nearly there. Hold on." If possible, his voice gained another layer of tender on top of the gravel-filled demand.

"Okay." Her eyes sank closed, and she floated down into the exhausting and blistering cold.

SECRET SANTA

Chapter Fourteen

Truck

"Kitt, I need you to open the door." The boy moved to do that, stepping back to hold the screen wide and Truck pushed past the only partially closed inside door. "Where's the bathtub, son? We need to warm your momma up."

She was so cold, and had gone still over the last mile, her body loose-limbed in his arms. He hadn't really been worried about hypothermia until her speech had turned delirious, then he realized she had stopped shivering, the clicking of her teeth ceasing as she fled consciousness.

Kitt led the way up the stairs and Truck used the heel of his boot to push the front door shut before following. They turned right at the top of the stairs and into what looked like the master bedroom and Truck paused a moment, taking in the only room in the house that held character. Decorated in warm, rich colors and fabrics, it held a large, tall bed covered in plush blankets and throw pillows. The walls were covered in paintings and pictures, and he knew he would enjoy spending time in here plucking at the threads of his Vanna's personality, learning what made her tick.

First you need to warm her up, he heard and grinned. "Warm her up, and wake her up," he said aloud, agreeing with Tish for once.

"Present," Kitt said, stopping in the middle of the room and holding out the object in his hand, tattered paper nearly gone; the black rectangle bearing only a few remaining scraps. Truck looked down to see Kitt's muddy feet had left a smudged trail all the way across the polished wood of the floor.

Shit, Truck thought, *got two to warm up*. "Kitt, son, can you go get yourself some warm, dry, clean clothes?"

I got this one, Tish said, and Kitt turned to the door, again cradling the item he had carried so cautiously through the woods. "Present." His tone was aggrieved, but he moved out of sight and down the hallway.

Truck called after the boy, "Bring your clothes back here, Kitt. Hang out with me while we get Mom warmed up."

"PRESENT!" The bellow from a distance away made Vanna shift in his arms, and he continued on his path to the door that he hoped led to an adjoining bath.

Looking around the little room, he saw a wide, long bathtub lining the far wall, a separate shower stall arranged at one end. A short wall served as a divider, with the stool on the other side. Cabinets were built into the wall behind the door, and he saw decorative towels hanging from a rod near the sink. This was another area with a definite stamp of personality, and he chuckled to see the whimsical mermen paintings that hung on either side of the vanity mirror. His Vanna enjoyed a bit of fantasy it seemed, if the unrealistic bulging muscles and pecs on the fish-tailed men were any indication. *I'd give her whatever fantasy she needed*, he thought, cautiously reaching out to twist the tub's faucet handles, releasing a flood of water, carefully balancing his burden.

The sound reminded him of his terror as he ran beside her towards the creek, imagination feeding him visions of a struggling Kitt fighting chin-deep in raging waters. The outcome could have been so different, and this possibility was something he knew Vanna lived with every day with her boy. Trying to decipher his wants and needs from the limited clues he could provide. She lived her life in anticipation of the next demand. Always on duty, it seemed.

Fingers in the heating water, he tugged the tub stopper in place, seeing the level immediately begin to rise. He had just sat back on his haunches when he heard the rumble of an approaching vehicle and waited, listening to see if it passed by her house. When the engine noise swelled and cut off, he knew it must have pulled into her driveway. *She might have called someone before she chased after Kitt*, he thought, then discarded the idea. She'd run out of the house without shoes, without grabbing her phone, and without closing her door, there was no way she'd stopped to make a call.

"CADE!" Kitt's happy shout split the air and then Truck heard the boy's feet pelting back down the stairs, accompanied by Tish's laughter in his head. *Boy's got sweatpants on him at least*, she said and Truck shook his head at how his mind filled in her humor.

Sounds like it's someone he knows, Truck thought. Listening to the commotion of multiple people moving around on the ground floor, chatter and laughter interspersed with what sounded like concerned inquiries. Not willing to wait any longer to get Vanna into the water, he settled her into the warmth, keeping a hand behind her head, one tucked under her arm, supporting and holding her in place.

He narrowed his eyes when he recognized one of the voices filling the downstairs with loud demands. Tipping his head towards the door he shouted, "Gunny, man, *upstairs*." Heavy footsteps pounded up the stairs, followed by the now-familiar tread of Kitt, and another set he suspected belonged to Sharon.

"What the fuck?" Gunny's head stuck in the bathroom door, his gaze sweeping over Truck and Vanna. "The fuck are you doing in Peeper's bathroom, Truck?"

Truck turned back to a Vanna who had begun to rouse, the heat from the rising water finally beating back the chill. Mud and dirt swirled around her, twigs and leaves floating on top of the water and her thin t-shirt clung to every curve showing above the surface. *Beautiful curves*, he thought, his gaze tracing to the still-rising level of water and back up, *beautiful woman*.

Glancing back at Gunny, he made a quick decision to protect Kitt from knowing how his actions had endangered his mother, saying instead, "Kitt had a big morning. Went for a swim in the creek." He moved his feet slightly, conscious of his own wet socks and cold toes. "Vanna decided to join him." Her lashes fluttered against her cheeks, eyes peeking up at him in bemused surprise. "I need to get her warmed up, man. Can you and Sharon see to Kitt?"

Sharon's voice floated from behind him, concern warring with laughter in her tone. "Can do, Truck." Her voice turned wheedling, "Come on, Kitt. Let's get a shirt on you and warm socks. No seams, I know how you roll, buddy."

Shuffling footsteps were moving into the hallway when he heard Kitt say, uncertainty in his voice, "Cade?"

Without hesitation Sharon said, "You betcha, buddy. Cadence is sleeping on the couch, but we'll get you warm and then we'll set things up so you and she can play." Truck hadn't gotten a look at Sharon before she left Vanna's bedroom with Kitt, but she must have had her and Gunny's newest baby with her, because she continued, "And if you want to hold Kitten, we can arrange that, too."

Gunny's voice was rough with concern when he asked, "What the fuck happened, brother?"

"Kitt took a runner, tumbled into the creek." He shifted his hands, assisting Vanna in her efforts to sit up, feeling the occasional shivers still making their way through her. He sat back, trying not to smile when she glanced down to see the tips of her hardened nipples poking tents in her wet shirt, the transparent fabric doing nothing to hide the broad circles of her pebbled areolas. With a groan she lifted her arms and crossed them over her chest, not realizing she created cleavage he found just as delectable. Tongue tracing the inside of his lips, he waited until he could be sure his voice wouldn't give his arousal away before continuing, "Vanna fell while we were getting him out."

"And you're here because…" The tone of this question was hard, hanging in the air like an accusation. Gunny was protective of people he considered his responsibility, and from her stories last night Truck knew Vanna fell directly in that camp. He would need to tread as carefully with his brother as he had Kitt to ensure things stayed copacetic with Gunny.

"Bought a house down the road. As next door as it gets out here in the country. Vanna was gracious last night, offering use of her phone when I needed to make a call to the clubhouse and didn't have signal." He twisted, looking up at the big ex-Marine. "I get she's important to you, Gunny. I wouldn't disrespect the pictures on her wall, brother. Vanna's a beauty, inside and out, and I see she's more than a friend to you." Time to say things plain, make sure there're no misunderstandings. "I get it, brother. Much as it kills me, hell…much as I want to, I won't go there."

Laughter barked from Gunny's throat and he shocked Truck by saying, "Fuck, man. She wants you to go there, you'd be a fuckin' fool to pass this woman by."

A sound came from the tub and Truck turned back to see Vanna's head tipped to one side, her eyes on him. As he watched, one corner of her mouth curled up into a smile.

SECRET SANTA

Chapter Fifteen

Vanna

Is he saying what I think he's saying? The bemused thought flitted through her head as she stared up at Truck.

Gunny's laughter trailed off and she met his gaze over the top of Truck's head. "Peepers." He cleared his throat before continuing, "Momma, you sure you're okay?"

"Yeah, Lane." His mouth curved in a smile in response to hers. "I'm good."

"Want some coffee?"

It was her turn to chuckle and she nodded as she responded, "That would be perfect, son."

"Right on. You got it." Gunny tapped the doorframe twice, then twice again before ducking out and into her bedroom. She listened until she heard his voice join Sharon's downstairs, then turned to look at Truck, still kneeling beside the tub.

As she stared at him, thoughts of their evening rolled through her head. His laughter at her stories, the way he held her in his sleep, how well they fit together. Dancing with him. The unhappy look in his eyes when he misunderstood her words this morning. How it had hurt to let him walk out the door, thinking in her pain that she was simply being maudlin again. Discounting what she felt.

Then there was his sudden and miraculous appearance in the woods, helping her hold it together so she could think, then his headlong dash across the field as he rushed to save her son. How he coaxed Kitt home, speaking soft encouraging words to her son while she listened with eyes closed, suspended securely in his arms. He was the same man with or without an audience. Good and kind, caring and supportive. *And he kinda just said he wants me*, she thought.

Lips pressed together, the expression on his face somber, he stared back at her. *He's about to do something really stupid. Don't let him say goodbye*, a thought not her own flitted through her head and she jerked, then blurted an unexpected question, "You sorta like me?"

He blinked and his mustache moved, cheeks lifting his lips into a smile. "Yeah, darlin'. I sorta do."

Still unfiltered, she heard her voice say, "I like you, too." He blinked again, and his mouth opened but she forestalled whatever he had been about to say when she continued, "Sorta a lot. Like, not even sorta. Just a lot."

Truck moved, his hand gliding up her shoulder as he lifted it to cup her jaw. Leaning in, he brushed his lips across hers. Coming back for a second pass, still gentle, then he pressed in, as in *pressed in*, molding his mouth to hers in a way that demanded a response. She kissed him back, his face slowly fading from view as her eyes slipped closed. The roar of the water rushing from the faucet drowned out the other sounds in the room for long minutes. No one could hear how his exploration of her mouth evoked soft moans. Her gasps as their tongues were slipping and sliding, tangling deliciously. "I amend my previous statement," he murmured when he finally pulled back a fraction, lips still touching hers, beard tickling her skin. "I don't sorta like you. I just like you. A lot."

Head tipped back, resting on the edge of the tub, she felt the loss of his hand then heard the water cut off and she knew where it went. Quickly it was back, stroking down her throat, curving around her shoulder as he lifted her to meet his mouth again. Her fingers glided up his arm, and she let her thumb caress his rough, bearded jaw. Feeling the muscles flex and move under her touch as he kissed her, wet and deep, eating down her moans with an open, hungry mouth. She stretched, moving up, fingers sliding into his hair, tangling on the tie holding it back and away from his face.

His hand shifted, palm covering her breast and this time it was she who took his reaction in, his deep groan rattling down her throat as his powerful fingers flexed and tightened, gentle as they caressed her. "*God*, Vanna," he said, his voice holding that rough edge she hadn't recognized as passion before.

Kitt shouted from downstairs and she smiled, feeling Truck's lips curving against hers in reply. "I think I should pretend to be a good hostess. Kitt's a lot to take when he's this excited."

"Shar's got this," he told her, but he slowly released his grip, shifting back to sit on his heels. "You get warmed up before you climb out, darlin'." Reaching out, he trailed one thumb across her lips, gaze tracing the path with a heated look. "If you're steady now, I'll let you get cleaned up. I'll see you downstairs?"

This last was a question, and she knew it was his way of being sure she wanted him there when she came downstairs. "You better, mister. I know where you live, you know. I can hunt you down." His shouted laughter rang loud in the small room, and she smiled up at him as he caressed her face one last time before leaving.

SECRET SANTA

Chapter Sixteen

Truck

Never would have expected this to be my Christmas day, he thought, looking around Vanna's kitchen. Gunny and Sharon stood to one side, Gunny with beer in hand because he'd informed Vanna that skunky or not, if there was beer he'd be drinking it. Kitt was next to them, but ass to the floor, legs straight out, the toddler Cadence holding his hands for balance as she stood on his thighs. Knees bending, her body was rocking back and forth in a dance to music it seemed only she and Kitt could hear, because his head tipped back and forth in time.

He had hurried, but Vanna had already been downstairs before he returned from heading through the woods to his house for a change of clothes. When he walked in carrying his duffle, she smiled at him, reaching her hand out to take the bag from his suddenly nervous grip, tossing it to Kitt with a quiet request to take up and put in her bedroom.

Vanna was tucked against his side, nice and tight so his arm could wrap around her and hold her in place. She and Sharon hadn't stopped talking for more than a minute, and he glanced down as she laughed, her head tipping back so she caught his gaze. Dipping his head, he brushed his mouth against hers, feeling the heat and silk of her lips.

Gunny interrupted, saying loudly, "Saw nobody opened the packages I fuckin' wrapped and mailed. What the hell, Peepers? You slackin' on Christmas, woman?"

Kitt's head straightened at Gunny's words and he pulled Cadence close, eyes fixed on her face as he whisper-shouted, "Presents. Cade, *presents*." Looking up at his mother, he told Vanna, "Now, presents."

"Yes, Kitt. We can open presents now."

Gunny scooped up a laughing Cadence and they all made their way into the dining room. Kitt repeated the earlier scene, demanding everyone sit on the floor near the tree while he shook his head at Truck, putting the Santa hat on a laughing Gunny's head this time.

There were more presents under the tree than before, and Kitt's face twisted in confusion until Sharon explained, "We brought our Christmas with us, buddy." She handed a sleeping Kitten to Vanna and scooted a little closer. "I'll help you. We'll sort things out."

She and Kitt made quick work, creating six piles of packages, then Kitt surprised Truck when he placed the sodden rectangle to one side, patting it. "Truck." Kitt kept his hand on it for a moment, then looked at Truck, his expression severe as he said, "Wait."

"Okay, son, I'll wait," he replied and Kitt held his version of a lock on their gaze, eyes cutting up and down, glancing away and back, away and back before holding a moment longer. Then his eyes darted to the rest of the packages.

Twenty minutes later nearly all the packages had been opened, paper and ribbons discarded in a flurry of tearing and shouts of joy. Cadence had abandoned the action early and was now seated nearby in a large box, happily playing with the set of brightly-colored building blocks she'd received.

Kitt held the last package with his name on it, and Truck felt Vanna tense beside him. Looking at her he saw her lips had rolled to a thin line, drawn between her teeth in her nervousness. "What is it?" he whispered his question and without looking up she answered, her voice low and uneasy.

"A promise."

Kitt had one long edge of the box pried open, tape torn away when he suddenly stopped and looked at the black case beside him. Dropping his package, letting it land in a noisy jangle in his lap, he leaned over and picked up what Truck now realized was an electronic tablet in a thick case. The boy's fingers worked the buttons on the side as Kitt woke it up. *Oh man, it took a bath in the creek*, Truck thought, hoping that case was waterproof.

Kitt's motions were deft as he called up an app, then stopped and stared at the tablet for a moment before extending it to Truck. "Present." Kitt's fingers didn't let go, though, his eyes flicking up and down, catching and releasing Truck's gaze a half-dozen times before Kitt finally relaxed his grip. This was important to him, his present to Truck. Kitt's voice was soft when he spoke, his face expressing how much he saw and knew, even if he found it hard to express. "Vanna Mom's Santa."

Turning the device so he and Vanna could look at it, Truck's breath caught in his throat as Vanna's fingers clutched tight on his thigh. On the screen was an image of him and Vanna. Standing close, he held her in his arms as they danced in the living room last night. The picture captured them in mid-laugh, his head angled down and hers up, intently looking into each other's face, identical expressions of happy discovery in place. He remembered thinking that he would gladly do the same thing every Christmas Eve if given the chance. So much possibility captured in this image, it was a promise of its own. The potential of a full, rich life filled with laughter and love.

Truck turned his head to study Vanna seated beside him, her fingers wound around his leg and she raised one hand, fingertips tracing his face on the screen. Lifting her gaze to meet his, she offered him a tremulous smile and he reached out, cupping her cheek in his palm, loving how even in this small way she fit him. "Beautiful," he said softly, brushing his thumb across those lips he so wanted to kiss. "Santa's Vanna."

"DOG!" Kitt's excited shout cut through the moment, jerking Vanna's attention to the side and Truck took advantage of her distraction to lean forward, his hand bringing her face back to his so he could press his mouth to hers. "DOG!" Kitt had finished opening the last present and was excitedly clambering over Vanna's lap to get to Truck, dangling a brilliant blue collar and leash in his face. "DOG!"

"Getting' a dog, Kitt?" He asked, grinning to see Kitt's head bob up and down in a vigorous nod. "What kind of dog?" Kitt's eyes widened, and he twisted to look at Vanna, the question echoed in his gaze.

"Brutus got a girlfriend," she told Kitt and the boy hooted. Turning to Truck she said, "Brutus is Blackie's Great Dane." He nodded, because he had met Brutus more than once. Stories for another day. *There'll be another day*, he heard, *I see good things*. "We'll go pick her up in a week, honey. Seven wakeups."

"Nope," Gunny drawled, shoving up from where he sat on the floor, torn pieces of paper fluttering from his tree trunk legs. "Just so happens we swung through Texas on our way."

Chapter Seventeen

Kitt

Chin down, Kitt looked again at the picture on his tablet. Truck knew without being told the tablet wasn't the present, the picture was. Vanna Mom and Truck. Without raising his head, he let his eyes wander across the floor, seeing Gunny stretched out flat of his back, Kitten lifted high as he swooped her side-to-side, child and man laughing. *Airplane*, he thought, his insides shivering, *scary*. Gunny's head was in Sharon's lap, and Cade was leaning against her Sharon Mom's side, fingers playing with her long hair.

Cutting his gaze the other direction, he saw two pairs of socked feet resting close together on the ottoman, legs extending to the couch where Vanna Mom sat right beside Truck. His arm was around her shoulder and Kitt liked how that looked. Liked how it made him feel inside. Hot and cold, because if Vanna Mom was happy it meant he could stop worrying she would be alone. He didn't know what to think when he woke up last night, but after seeing them dancing he knew. *I see good things*, he thought, twisting to look at the gangly puppy curled up beside his leg.

Chapter Eighteen

Kitt

Four Christmases later

Kitt glanced at his watch. Vanna Mom was late. Not frighteningly so. Not yet. But late was late and she didn't do late. He glanced across the table to where Truck Pops sat, hand to his mug of coffee, the other holding a book flat on the table. Turning a page, he settled his hand back onto the book, then lifted the coffee, sipping without looking up. Kitt looked down at the tablet on the table in front of him, his book waiting patiently for his attention to return, no need to hold his place. Clock at the top glaring out the time.

Since anime had captured his attention two years ago, he and Truck Pops had many discussions about their favorite ways to consume information. *The tablet was far superior*, he thought. *Better, greater, excellent, first-rate.*

Stop it, he scolded himself.

Glancing around the kitchen, Kitt took in the changes in their décor, something that he would have never noticed even a year ago, unless it disturbed him. Vanna Mom had known this, had known that misaligned edges or clashing colors set up a resonance inside him, that resulting vibration making it so he couldn't think, couldn't breathe some days, so she had kept their house a safe place. A resting place.

The walls were no longer empty. *Different*, he thought, *but okay*. He'd come home from Blackie's last summer with a painted plate to hang. He and Randi, Blackie's girl who was also his friend, but not his girlfriend, had painted it. Elias, who wasn't Blackie's son, but was Randi's boyfriend in the way Kitt wasn't even though Blackie said she would never be old enough to have a boyfriend, was there too, and while Kitt's plate held a rooster, Elias' plate was a lizard.

"I like roosters better," he said, gaze swinging to the wall of roosters decorating the kitchen. One wall out of four, the others left bare and he was often grateful for that space to rest his eyes. But, he liked the roosters, too. "Lots of roosters." All different kinds. Plates and plaques, iron and wood, big and small, old and new. One a clock, a feather from the rooster's tail the sweeping minute hand, pointing out the same thing his watch and tablet had told him. "Vanna Mom's late."

A reassuring rumble rolled across the room, warmth settling into his chest from the care and concern carried on that wave. "She called, son. Unavoidably detained, but she'll be here within thirty minutes of when she called. You talked to her. Twenty minutes ago. She'll be here soon." Truck Pops reminded him of something he should have remembered and Kitt frowned. It happened less often now, but sometimes he misplaced things like that. Chin to his chest, he looked down at the tablet, seeing it had gone to sleep. *Like my brain*.

A rough tap woke it, an impatient swipe unlocked it. A touch to his leg made him take a breath, only realizing then that he was holding onto the air in his lungs. *Trachea, bronchus, diaphragm. Aveoli, pleura, bronchioles, lobes*.

Stop it, he shouted in his head. He didn't get as lost inside himself now, not as much as before, but it frustrated him when he couldn't stop the thoughts from tumbling down the pathways in his mind. That touch came again, followed by a pressure on top of his thigh and he looked down, seeing mismatched eyes staring up at him. Blue and brown. Black and white. *Charity*.

Now his mind carried a sing-song tune with the words he spun next, but he didn't mind these, because his friend was every one of these to him. *Goodness, mercy, beauty. Kindness, compassion, love.* "Love." Easy and natural, his muscles relaxed as he lifted a hand to Charity's head, cupping her skull in his palm, feeling the heat radiating from her brain. Her brainbox worked so hard. Eyebrows moving up and down, she kept her worried gaze on him, loose lips drooling on his jeans. *I got this*, he thought. *I see good things*, she told him without words.

Brain untangled, he found his words to tell Truck what he was thinking. "Mom's never late. Is it the apartment?" Next Monday was M-Day. Moving day, Monday. Atlanta was big and scary. Trains and busses everywhere, cars everywhere, people everywhere. Loud people. Smelly people. So many people. Pressure on his leg, a warm swipe of a tongue along the inside of his wrist let his lungs start working again.

His thumb moved across the skin of Charity's head, silken and smooth, the texture always pleasing under his fingers. Black and white, a patternless-pattern he had traced thousands of times. A thing that should have been certain to make him anxious allowing him to camouflage that anxiety within the pattern, hiding it from sight every time she pressed up against him. *Harlequin. Clown. Jester. Charity.*

MariaLisa deMora

He pressed play on the memory in his head, like he'd tap an app on the tablet, hearing Vanna Mom—*Mom*, he corrected himself—telling him about the apartment. Patiently going over things for the kajillionth time with him because he wanted to make sure he had it right.

"It's a nice house, Kitt. A really nice house. Remember what it looked like from our visit? Half of the second floor is yours and your neighbor is a young man about your age. Pete has Down's Syndrome, so you'll have to take care with his feelings. His name is Pete."

"Pete," he said, then looked up, realizing Truck Pops—*Pops*, he corrected himself—had said something. "Sorry?"

"Nothing's happened with the apartment, Kitt. We're still right on track with everything. No holding back there, you're moving in next week." Truck lifted a hand in a silent question and Kitt nodded, breathing easier when it settled on his shoulder. Heat flowed through him from that connection, meeting the heat from his hand on Charity somewhere in the middle, working together to unravel his words again.

"I worry. Not about Mom." Eyes to the table, he still knew Pops' face changed, softened when he admitted that wasn't a concern anymore. Pops understood a lot without Kitt's words, had known from the beginning that his worst fear was Mom would be alone. He needed to figure out how to live in the world as it

107

swirled around him, and he was excited about that chance, but worried because he was all she had once. "She's got you now." Fingers squeezing tight on his shoulder, anchoring him like the constant pressure on his thigh from Charity's head. "She needed you, Pops."

"I think we needed each other, son." Kitt nodded, glancing up to see Pops' eyes pointing his way. Glancing down and back up, he nodded again. Pops dipped his face, making a point to lock his gaze on Kitt's face when he said, "I needed you, too, Kitt." Charity's eyes, one mottled brown and one crystal blue, stared up at him. She licked the inside of his wrist again, the rasping swipe of warmth reassuring.

"Charity will miss the house." *I'm going to miss the house*. Flicking his gaze around the room, he settled on the wall of color. "The roosters."

"Mark which ones you want to take with you," Pops said immediately, understanding without judging. "We'll get a special box to put them in, make sure they travel well. Set them up first thing so you can see them."

Kitt nodded, glad beyond anything he could ever hope to communicate that this man came to their house four Christmas Eves ago. Glancing up, he gave Pops a grin, not even one he had to practice in the mirror, trying hard not to look into his own eyes because that was the worst. Seeing himself the way

MariaLisa deMora

other people saw him, all sticking-up hair and anxious eyes, lips that didn't know what to do with themselves, hands that were worse with the not-knowing. Not the him he knew he was inside. But a grin that came easily was good and right, and that's what he had right now. Good and right. "Presents tomorrow."

"Yeap, presents tomorrow. Know which one you want to open first?" Kitt twisted in his chair, dislodging Charity's head to look at the tree. She groaned her disapproval and immediately reclaimed her place, moving from under the table to his side to do so.

"Smallest." There was a tiny package hanging from one branch of the tree and he thought he knew what it was. Not that he'd ever tell Mom he'd figured it out, but he was sure it held a key and keyring. *My apartment*, he thought. *A promise*, he heard in his head, that woman's voice coming less frequently in past months, still reassuring. *Yeah*, he told her. *A promise from Mom to me.* "You?"

Pops' response was lost in the sound of a car coming down the road and Charity's ears perked up, her tilted head aimed at the door. Not barking, which meant, "MOM."

"Sounds like it. She's going to have groceries, but give her a minute to hide anything she doesn't want us to see." Christmas meant secrets, but not bad ones. Good ones. Ones you had to let the other person have, even if it made your brain crazy with thinking and wondering. Secrets he could keep better next year.

"Christmas year next could be mine." A tree in his apartment. Twisting to look at the one in the dining room, he tilted his head like Charity did sometimes. "Not big." Swinging back to Pops, he grinned, right and good again. "Mine."

"You got it, if Mom's good with the idea. Christmas at your place next year. Small tree doesn't mean small celebration." Pops grinned back at him, lips lifting the beard framing his mouth, round glasses perched on his nose because he'd been reading. "Sounds like a plan."

Later that night Kitt sat on the stairs in what had become his favorite perch, staring through the railing at his mom and a fulfilled promise. A promise Pops fulfilled every year when he did this. The scratching sounds came from the record player, then music filled the air, soft and sweet, soothing. Christmastime wouldn't be scary, not even in the city, not according to these words. There'd be people, but Mom and Pops wouldn't let him be alone to be afraid. Heat radiating from beside him, he reached out to lay a hand on Charity's back, feeling the rumble of her groaning approval.

In the living room, the parents he loved more than he could ever say swayed together, moving to the music as they had so often since Pops knocked on their door. These were the good things he had seen that long ago

MariaLisa deMora

night, the promise of love and a family. Charity leaned into him and he gave her a hug. Big and solid, she made things better. Another promise fulfilled.

From the kitchen he heard the brief crow of a rooster, signaling midnight. With a grin, he watched as Pops' head dipped down, kissing Mom. He had to wait a long time before they were done. Before he saw them looking at each other like they always did, as if the joy and love they found there were a pleasant surprise. He waited another minute, letting the song wind down to quiet before he did what he always did.

"PRESENTS!"

111

Merry Christmas to all of you!

~ML

THANK YOU FOR READING
SECRET SANTA!

Thank you for reading *Secret Santa*, the free short story for 2016, lining up as #9.75 in the **Rebel Wayfarers MC** series. A story that is personal and close to my heart, I hope this is a conversation starter for many people.

You can find out more about Erin Hanson, the Australian poet mentioned in the acknowledgements, on her website: thepoeticunderground.com

ABOUT THE AUTHOR

Raised in the south, MariaLisa learned about the magic of books at an early age. Every summer, she would spend hours in the local library, devouring books of every genre. Self-described as a book-a-holic, she says "I've always loved to read, but then I discovered writing, and found I adored that, too. For reading...if nothing else is available, I've been known to read the back of the cereal box."

Also by MariaLisa deMora

Alace Sweets

A dark thriller, this book is not a light read. Filled with edge-of-your-seat suspense, this intense story commands the reader's attention as it drives towards the explosive ending. Alace Sweets is a vigilante serial killer, with everything that implies and is sure to trip all your triggers. Be ready.

At seventeen, Alace Sweets turned a corner in her life, taking the wrong shortcut home from school.

Resisting the harsh knowledge her attackers will never be made to pay for their actions, Alace takes a stand. Justice must be served, and if fate's scales are out of balance, she's determined to set things right as best she can.

When the laws of men fail, the rules of Alace prevail.

5-Star Reviews for Alace Sweets

"deMora has a superb story-line and exceptional character development. All of her characters have such depth that will intrigue the reader..."
~Turning Another Page

"Hot, sweet, dark thriller."
~Beth D

"It will keep you on the edge of your seat and give you chills."
~Escape Reality Book Blog

"Disturbing, haunting, sickly; yet hot, sexy and heart racing!"
~Amanda L

"From the first page [deMora] pulls you into the world she has created and you do not even try to escape..."
~Little Shop of Readers Blog

"A must read for all those dark, gritty romance fans out there."
~Sweet & Spicy Reads

"You will find yourself so drawn into the story that the outside world is blocked out and your locking the doors and turning on all the lights."
~Danena F

"Don't judge me for bonding with a vigilante serial killer, she's more than what she does."
~iScream Books

"Thrilling...chilling...full of suspense, nail biting edge of your seat excitement."
~Tracey H

"Every time MariaLisa deMora picks up her pen (or opens her computer), she creates characters you want to believe in."
~Gail S

"Intriguing dark storyline, beautiful love story and nail-biting conclusion, what more could a reader ask for?"
~Manda M

"This is my favourite book so far from this author ... I recommend this book if you enjoy dark romantic thrillers."
~Cheekypee Reads and Reviews

"There's not enough stars to give this book and 5 just doesn't really do it justice!"
~DeLane C

"I couldn't put this book down from page one! Tried to stop & go to bed but couldn't sleep thinking about Alace and got up & finished the book."
~Debbie M

"This book takes you a dark and twisted ride that is gripping..."
~Renee Entress' Blog

"This book is dark and gritty and I literally had to take a day off from reading it because it's that intense."
~My Girlfriend's Couch

"MariaLisa DeMora, wordsmith that she is, made this a story of the enlightenment of a woman and finding love in a life where she has had none."
~Kat W

"Whatever deep dark trench [deMora] pulled a character like Alace from should be revisited again and often."
~Confessions of a Serial Reader

ADDITIONAL SERIES AND BOOKS

Please note that books in a series frequently feature characters from additional books within that series. If series books are read out of order, readers will twig to spoilers for the other books, so going back to read the skipped titles won't have the same angsty reveals.

Rebel Wayfarers MC series:

Mica, #1
A Sweet & Merry Christmas, short story #1.5
Slate, #2
Bear, #3
Jase, #4
Gunny, #5
Mason, #6
Hoss, #7
Harddrive Holidays, short story #7.5
Duck, #8
Biker Chick Campout, short story #8.5
Watcher, #9

A Kiss to Keep You, novella #9.25
Gun Totin' Annie, short story #9.5
Secret Santa, short story #9.75
Bones, #10
Gunny's Pups, novella #10.25
Never Settle, short story #10.5
Not Even A Mouse, short story #10.75
Fury, #11
Christmas Doings, #11.25
Gypsy's Lady, #11.5
Cassie, #12
Road Runner's Ride, novella #12.5

Occupy Yourself band series:

Born Into Trouble, #1
Grace In Motion, #2 (TBD)
What They Say, #3 (TBD)

Neither This, Nor That series:

This Is the Route Of Twisted Pain, #1
Treading the Traitor's Path: Out Bad, #2
Trapped by Fate on Reckless Roads, #3 (TBD)

Other Books:

With My Whole Heart
Alace Sweets
Hard Focus

More information available at mldemora.com.